A Husband For Christmas

Nancy Pirri

To Mom and Dad.
I miss you every day.

CHAPTER 1

St. Paul Minnesota
September 1946

Captain Jack Campbell, a schooled architect and accountant, and a medic during the war, honorably discharged from the United States Army, sat on the doctor's examination table, wondering if his leg would ever heal completely.

Dr. Richardson gave him an answer without Jack having to ask. "The leg's better than I expected, Jack. But I'm afraid you'll have a permanent limp for the rest of your life from the lodged shrapnel."

Jack shrugged. "Guess dancing's out for me."

"You'll be able to manage the ones that count...the slow ones." He gave Jack a sly look. "Bet you can't wait to hold a pretty girl in your arms for a night of dancing. You were gone nearly three years, weren't you?"

Jack nodded. "Yes, it's good to be back in familiar territory."

Dr. Richardson's smile slipped. "Have you been home yet? Seen your father?"

"No. He doesn't want to see me. I met my mother for lunch last week, though. She, at least, appreciates the fact I survived the war."

"He'll get over you enlisting, sooner or later. Don't think badly of him. You are, after all, his only child. And now that you've returned you can take up the reins of the family business."

"Father threatened to will the business to a distant cousin, if I enlisted. I'd never wanted to make a career out of the steel business anyway, so I gave him my blessing."

"Think that's a wise move?"

"It's the smartest one I've ever made, Doc."

"So, what are your plans?"

"I'm going to return to LaSalle National Bank as head accountant. Then I'm going to search for a woman willing to be my wife and bless me with children. I've seen friends die and know life can be too short."

The doctor frowned. "I heard you'd made marriage plans before leaving for the war."

"Things never worked out between Veronica and me."

He heard bitterness in his voice when he thought about his ex-fiancée. Thought how he'd received letters from friends about how she'd been seen around the city with an old friend of his, Sedrick Hawthrone. She'd never even had the decency to write him a 'Dear John' letter while he was in the army but had simply stopped replying to his own.

"Veronica Miller wasn't your style, son. Bah! Society girls are nothing but spoiled debutantes with no brain inside their pretty little heads. You need a smart woman, one who's independent and can think for herself; a woman who can be a helpmate, not a noose around your neck. Besides, there are plenty of ladies around who'd be proud to marry a war hero, who also happens to be a millionaire."

Dryly, Jack said, "I won't inherit that money until I marry. And if I don't marry and get my millions, well, it'll only mean

I'll have to work a while longer at the bank to save up enough money to launch my business. My grandmother and her will —it's ridiculous."

"Your granny sure knew how to rile things up when she was alive, but now she's doing it from the grave, too." The doctor chuckled. "She was a hell of a gal."

"If it hadn't been for my mother wanting me home in one piece, I probably would have stayed in the army, and to hell with those millions. It's tough being an only child."

"Yeah, real tough," the doctor said with a laugh, slapping Jack's back.

Jack left the doctor's office and limped down the street to his new model Studebaker, noticing dames of all shapes and sizes sending appreciate glances his way. He had gained twenty pounds of muscle while serving his country, so none of his pre-service clothes fit him. Home for nearly a month, he still hadn't had a chance to have new clothes made so he still wore his Army uniform.

He started thinking about his long-range business goals and smiled, knowing he was on the right track. Soldiers were getting married every day with the ending of the war, and there was a definite housing shortage. The home-building industry was set to explode, even though his father still felt steel was the clear ticket to success.

Perhaps he was right, but Jack had never had the interest his father had in the steel mining business. He also recalled how his father would be gone for weeks at a time, running his business, traveling and selling, leaving Jack and his mother alone. Jack had long ago decided he'd work no more than nine to five at his business and spend the rest of his time surrounded by his lovely, loving wife and children.

At twenty-nine, he was ready to find the right woman to marry and settle down to a normal work schedule, unlike his father. A sweet, compliant, pretty woman with a sensible head on her shoulders would be a good companion for him; one who cared more for him more than society events. A woman who wouldn't mind keeping a home and caring for children and having him be the provider; fulfilling his needs would be enough for his wife.

Rose Delaney sat in her boss's office, fingers twisting the corner of her handkerchief, wet with her tears.

"Mrs. Delaney," Mr. Jorgenson said carefully, "a woman's place is in the home, unless there's a war on. You were fully aware of the fact you'd lose your job once Jack Campbell returned from active duty."

Disappointment settled deep inside Rose but somehow, she managed to keep her voice calm. "What am I supposed to do? I've a child at home to support, and no husband."

"I'm so sorry," he murmured.

Rose didn't think he sounded a bit sorry though she saw color flood his cheeks. He continued, "LaSalle National Bank promised our men they'd be given their jobs back upon their return from the service, and you were informed about this when you took the job. Jack Campbell's a decorated war hero and is ready to return to work now that his injuries have healed. His position's the one you currently occupy."

"Is he married?" she daringly asked.

The benign smile he'd given her he replaced with a scowl. "I don't see why it's any concern of yours," he said, picking up a stack of papers from his desk and shuffling them.

"I do," Rose said, leaning toward him. "You see, I could understand him needing this job if he were married and had a family to support. If he's only responsible for himself, then I can't see why he can't find a job elsewhere and leave this one to me."

He rose from his chair and came around to the front of his desk. Taking her elbow in a light grasp he pulled her gently from her seat and walked her to the door. "I'm sorry. Your last day is the sixteenth of the month. I've a meeting in a few minutes. Perhaps we can find another position for you. Let me think on it."

In her office, she sank into the chair behind her desk. Her hand shook as she tried smoothing out her frizzy hair. What would she do now? How would she support herself and Sarah, her four-year old daughter? Then hope filled her. Perhaps Mr. Jorgenson could find another position for her, one that hopefully paid as well as her current job. She could only hope.

Her husband, Timothy, had been listed as missing in action, assumed to have died at Pearl Harbor, leaving her pregnant and jobless. Other than her neighborhood soda fountain waitress job she'd held as a teenager she hadn't worked upon graduating from high school. She'd attended business college for two years and studied accounting. But then she and Timothy had married. They'd spent just one night together—their wedding night, before he left for active duty. Six weeks later Rose discovered she was expecting a baby. Timothy never knew about the pregnancy, nor ever saw his daughter.

Rose's business college certificate was the reason she'd managed to secure a well-paying job at LaSalle National once America became involved in the war. The bank had been desperately seeking a head accountant and had been delighted to hire her—even if she'd been four months pregnant at the time. Now, with the return of a local war hero, they apparently had no qualms about letting her go.

Rose received a small widow's pension but that was all. Her home was a modest one-story with a quaint, enclosed front porch, which required many repairs she couldn't afford. Now she was faced with the dilemma of keeping up the mortgage without a decent paying job.

The next morning, after a neighbor with a child Sarah's

age picked her up in the family car to take Sarah to school as they did each school day, she dressed for work in one of three suits she'd purchased upon her hiring at LaSalle Bank. She felt extremely blessed that Sarah had been deemed with advanced intelligence and had been able to start kindergarten school a year earlier.

She pulled a navy serge suit from her closet. The jacket was double-breasted with well-padded shoulders, the skirt pencil-thin, emphasizing her trim figure. Her starched white blouse contrasted dramatically with the suit. She pinned a sapphire and diamond broach to one lapel, a wedding gift from Timothy, and stared at her reflection in the mirror positioned on the wall behind her dressing table.

Depression settled over her. She didn't feel like venturing outdoors where it had been raining for two days but knew she must. She still had her job and two weeks of pay coming. Quickly, she pulled on her raincoat, grabbed her umbrella from its stand then locked the front door.

It rained often in the fall in the Midwest, and on this cool morning torrents of rain fell from the sky, pounding the sidewalk and streets. As Rose stood on the corner a few blocks from her house, waiting for the streetcar to take her to work downtown St. Paul, a shiny, deep blue Studebaker screamed past her. Rose caught her breath as ice-cold water splashed up into her face, soaked her feet and plastered her seamed silk stockings to her legs.

The force of the wind made her struggle to keep the umbrella over her head. Once she was certain the umbrella was stable, she dug inside her pocket, found a damp handkerchief and swiped the water from her cheeks, trying not to disturb her makeup; trying not to bawl like a baby.

She heard the shriek of a car's wheels braking and looked up in time to see the Studebaker barreling toward her, in reverse. She jumped back from the curb, ready to flee when a man's solicitous deep voice called out to her.

"Sorry about that, miss! I didn't see you on the corner until the last minute. Can I give you a lift somewhere?"

Rose moved closer to the curb, bent down and peered at the man through the window he'd cranked open. His light brown hair was cut severely short on the sides, but long on top, his eyes deep blue and merry. His smile was wide, and flashing white teeth caught her attention. She was half-tempted to accept a ride but knew she couldn't. He was a stranger—a stranger who'd drenched her from head to toe, her raincoat and umbrella having afforded her little protection.

She heard rumbling and looked up to see the streetcar arriving. Brakes screeched as the vehicle came to a grinding halt behind the Studebaker. The streetcar driver honked at the man to move but he didn't budge.

"Come on! You're soaking wet," he shouted.

Rose's eyes widened on the passenger door he'd swung open. She shook her head as a nervous feeling sent prickles up her spine. It was broad daylight so she shouldn't be frightened. But there was something about the man's confidence and tone of voice that made her uneasy. Just the little he'd said led her to believe he was the type who wouldn't take 'no' for an answer.

"Yes, I'm wet, thanks to you!" she finally got the nerve to shout as she continued to back away. She ran for the streetcar, tore up the steps and found a seat right behind the driver.

"You okay, miss?" the driver asked as he peered at her in his mirror. "Was that guy pestering you?"

"I'm fine," Rose replied, her cheeks heating up.

The man *had* bothered her. He'd just made her aware of the fact she was, indeed, still a woman. Nearly five years had passed since Timothy left, and she hadn't had a single date since then. But then, other than young boys and elderly gentlemen, there hadn't been many eligible men around during the war years, not that she'd gone looking. To her mind she was still married—until Timothy's death could be proved.

She arrived at her destination, stepped off the streetcar and walked briskly up the street toward the bank building built of red brick and eight stories high. She took the stairs to the third floor, stopped in the ladies' room to check her makeup and comb her hair, which was hopeless. Her honey-blonde colored hair, which she'd painstakingly pin-curled to make it smoother was now an unruly mass of frizz surrounding her face. Her makeup was streaky and some of it had bled onto the once pristine white collar of her blouse. She groaned when she turned, glanced down at one leg and saw the run in her stocking. Hopefully, she still had an extra pair in her desk drawer.

Rose did the best she could with her appearance, then headed for her office. "Hello, Marianne," she said as she passed the receptionist.

The young woman's eyes widened. "What happened to you, Mrs. Delaney?"

As Rose moved toward her office, she said, "Let's just say I had an encounter with a Studebaker. Okay?"

"Uh, sure. Say, Mr. Jorgenson said you should come straight to his office."

"Let him know I'll be in shortly."

Marianne protested, "Oh, but he doesn't want you to go to your office until you've seen him first!"

Coming to an abrupt halt, Rose narrowed her eyes on Marianne. "Don't tell me he's cleared my things out already."

"Um, no, not yet, but…"

"Good, then my extra stockings should still be in my desk. Ring him and tell him I'll be there in five minutes."

She ignored Marianne's stammering, opened her door and came to an abrupt halt with a gasp. Her chair was turned to face the bank of windows overlooking the city. She saw a pair of chocolate brown pants legs crossed, oxford shoes on feet settled against the windowsill—shoes she guessed that likely cost more than a week's salary; then she heard a man's deep, laughing voice as he talked with someone on the telephone.

He must have heard her enter as he pulled his legs down and swiveled around to face her. She stared in wide-eyed amazement into a pair of astonished, laughing blue eyes—familiar eyes.

CHAPTER 2

"Gotta go. See you around six," he said.

Rose's heart skipped a beat when she recognized the man in the Studebaker. The man who'd splashed her while she waited for the streetcar. He wore a brown tweed jacket that fit his broad shoulders well, and a crisp white shirt. The jacket was open, and she noticed his crisp white shirt and tan-colored suspenders. He was tall and muscular, had great teeth, nice mouth…sensitive lips. She met his candid gaze as he hung up the telephone and rose from her chair. He moved around the desk and headed toward her, his gaze steady on her, his gait long and confident—until she noticed the slight limp. She recalled her boss mentioning the fact that her replacement had sustained some war injuries, though she admitted the limp didn't detract from his handsome looks.

Rose stood riveted in place in the open doorway. She tried moving her limbs to meet him but found she couldn't. He stopped directly in front of her. It was then she saw how his height dwarfed her own five foot two inches.

With his eyes on hers he took her right hand and squeezed it gently. "Tell me you aren't Mrs. Delaney," he said, smiling down at her.

Prickles of awareness crawled up Rose's spine, but she had the wherewithal to reply, "Sorry, but I am." With a sigh she added, "You're my replacement?"

He grinned. "Technically speaking, you were *my* replacement. I'm Jack Campbell." He swept an appreciative look over her, even as a chagrined expression crossed his face. "Sorry I drenched you earlier. I truly hadn't seen anyone on the corner as I sped past, until the last moment."

She realized he still held her hand. Her first instinct was to tug it away, but she refused to get into a tug-of-war. Tilting her head back she gave him a cool, long look. Instead of releasing her hand he eased closer and continued to stare into her eyes.

Rose's hand went limp in his, her breathing sped up and her heartbeat pounded. He smiled gently down at her then and her breath caught at the tender look in his eyes. As he released her hand she groaned inside at the loss of the sweet contact. Her gaze remained focused on him, and she watched him fold his hands behind his back and spread his legs in a military stance.

"I've been checking over your work," he said. "You've done an exceptional job since I've been gone. Thank you."

She waved her hand negligently. "Oh, no thanks needed. I did what needed to be done and earned my pay. Now, if you'll excuse me, Mr. Jorgenson wants to see me in his office."

"I'm also heading that way." He reached out and cupped her elbow.

Rose backed away from him. "Um, I need to do something first, so go on ahead."

"Oh, no need to worry about the work anymore, Mrs. Delaney."

"Excuse me," she said, her back stiffening, "I have two more weeks left."

"Not necessary. I've been given a clean bill of health from my doctor. Today is your last day. No need to worry, though.

You'll be receiving your full two weeks' pay." He grinned. "No more having to get up early and taking a streetcar downtown. I'm certain your husband will be happy to have you home minding the house again."

Rose narrowed her eyes and pondered the near-wistful tone in his voice. Obviously, he was a traditional male. She couldn't help but ask the same words her employer had said to her earlier, "Are you saying a woman's place is in the home?"

He nodded. "The home is a woman's natural domain. Jorgenson mentioned you're a mother. Now you'll be able to focus all your time and attention on your family."

She stared at him and crossed her arms by way of a reply.

He frowned. "Why do I get the distinct impression this idea of home, hearth and family doesn't appeal to you?"

Was that disappointment she heard in his voice? And, if it was, why would he care about how she felt, anyway? She opened her mouth to let him know she was the soul-supporter of her family but stopped when the telephone buzzed. She walked around him and picked up the phone.

"Yes, Mr. Jorgenson, I'll be right there." She listened a moment longer then said, her voice sounding bitter to her own ears, "Yes, I've met Mr. Campbell. I'll bring him with me, of course." She hung up the phone, turned and saw Jack's gaze focused on her calves.

"You've a run in your stocking," he murmured. "Hope it wasn't because of me."

"Of course you didn't cause it," she reassured him. "Would you do me a favor?"

His eyes met hers. "Sure thing."

"Would you please tell Mr. Jorgenson I'll be there shortly? I'd like to change my stockings." She felt her cheeks heat up as his gaze swept up and down her body. He looked up then and met her scowl.

"Certainly," he said roughly, pivoted on his heel and left the office.

She locked her office door then retrieved a pair of nylons from her bottom desk drawer. While removing her torn stockings she wondered about the fleeting moment of embarrassment she'd seen on Mr. Campbell's face. She got the distinct impression he wasn't used to a woman's accoutrements, yet she believed he knew women well. She frowned though when she thought about his telephone conversation upon entering her office. Had he been speaking to a man or a woman? Whomever it was, from the repartee she'd heard, he'd felt comfortable with the person.

Quickly, she changed her stockings, walked down the hall and giving a short knock, immediately entered Mr. Jorgenson's office, feeling much more confident. There was nothing worse than a run in a stocking to undermine her image as a confident, capable businesswoman.

Jack rose from his chair, allowing her to sit. He took up a position against one wall, folding his arms across his chest and watching her with a grim expression.

"Jack here thought we could spare you and allow you to leave as of today, but I need you here a bit longer," her boss explained. Elation filled her soul at his words, but then promptly dissipated when he added, "I expect you to update Jack on what's been happening in the accounting department over the next few weeks."

"Oh, well, I..." Rose stumbled over her words, not certain how to reply when Jack entered into the conversation.

"I've already checked through some of the ledgers and don't think it'll be difficult for me to pick up from where Mrs. Delaney left off," he said smoothly. "Besides, I'm sure her husband wants her home after being in the work force for so long."

Stan Jorgenson cleared his throat, his face flushed pink. "Uh, pardon me for my bluntness, Mrs. Delaney." He looked at Jack. "Mrs. Delaney lost her husband in the war."

Tears prickled behind Rose's eyes. Even after all these years the mention of Timothy made her feel melancholy.

Mr. Campbell appeared uncomfortable at the news: his brow deeply furrowed. "I'm sorry," he said. "You should have said something earlier."

"I can't see it's any business of yours," Rose retorted. She looked at her boss. "Mr. Campbell is right to assume he should have no problems picking up where I left off. If he does have any questions, he may reach me at home. Now, gentlemen, if you'll excuse me, I'll pack up my things."

"But…now wait just a minute!" her boss protested.

"Yes, let's not be hasty," Jack said, stepping toward her.

Rose ignored them and made her way to her office, fuming inside. *Men!* She closed the door, went to a closet and pulled out an empty box. She started removing personal items from her desk drawers. She heard the door open and looked up to find Mr. Campbell standing there with a frown on his face. Even with the frown he was a handsome man, she decided as she waited for him to speak.

"We need to talk, Mrs. Delaney, although it seems silly for me to stand on such formality. Rose would be better, don't you think?"

"I prefer the formality as you and I will likely never cross paths again."

"Oh, I don't know about that. The bank's Christmas ball is in six weeks. I planned on asking you to attend as my guest."

"Horsefeathers," Rose said. "We hardly know each other."

"True, but I think we should remedy the problem— immediately. Since you're unattached I don't see any reason why we can't enjoy each other's company."

She raised her brow. "You're a regular Casanova, aren't you?"

His eyes narrowed. "What do you mean?"

She heard the cool tone in his voice but paid it no heed. "When I entered my office earlier weren't you on the phone?"

A crooked smile crossed his lips as he moved into the office and closed the door behind him. Casually, he leaned back against the door. "I was."

Rose nodded curtly. "I'm guessing with a woman?"

He nodded.

"Ask *her* to attend the Christmas ball with you." She started dumping her personal items into the box.

Frowning, he said, "Ask my mother? Why would I do that, much as I adore her? I'd much rather escort a beautiful woman like you."

She paused in her packing. "Your mother?"

He nodded. "That changes things, wouldn't you say?" He came around the side of her desk.

Rose froze when he stepped nearer, his eyes on hers. Her breathing grew shallow. Once he was right beside her, he tucked a frizzy strand of her hair behind her ear and she closed her eyes. At that moment, she realized how much she missed the intimacy between a man and a woman. Mentally, she shook herself, clearing her thoughts. Jack Campbell was a dangerously attractive man. How easily he'd tempted her.

She stepped back, returned to the box on her desk and closed it up. "I'm afraid not, Mr. Campbell. Sorry."

Why was she turning him down? Oh, there was no doubt in her mind she was attracted to him, but he was moving too fast. Also, she wasn't certain she wanted to form attachments with any man again at this point in her life, though Rose readily admitted to herself she had been lonely for male companionship since Timothy went into the service.

She was twenty-six, old enough to know what she wanted in life, but she wasn't certain she wanted to risk losing her heart again. She couldn't afford to live with that heartache, even though she had always longed to have more children.

Eventually, she'd have to take a chance on love again, or

be lonely for the rest of her life, knowing there were no guarantees of forever. And as the years passed, it looked more and more as though Timothy was truly gone.

Jack said, "Why not?"

She didn't reply but kept her head down, her hands busy with her work.

He laughed mirthlessly. "It's because of my limp, isn't it?"

Rose gasped and stared into his frowning visage. "No! I would never find fault with a man who'd honorably served his country as you have."

"Then, if it's not that, how come?"

She sighed. "Let's turn this conversation around. You tell me. Why are you asking me out? What do *you* want?"

He gave her a devilish smile and shrugged. "I haven't been on a date in nearly three years. Maybe I just want a bit of feminine companionship instead of a night out carousing with the guys."

"There are plenty of women who'd be happy to date you. Ask Marianne at the front desk."

"She's too young. Besides, I'm not interested in her." He sighed. "I'm moving too fast for you, aren't I?"

"Boy, you can say that again," she muttered.

"Give me your telephone number. I'd like to call you—get to know you better."

"By telephone?"

"Well, you won't let me take you out on a date. What's the real reason, Rose?"

"I'm just not interested." A voice inside her blared, Liar! Go out with the man.

"I don't believe you." He took her hand, kissed it again then settled it gently back on top of the box she'd been packing. His eyes were merry when he leaned close and whispered in her ear, "I'll be in contact soon."

After he left, her body started shaking like a leaf blowing in a gusty Minnesota wind. Desire shot through her from head to toe. Jack Campbell was handsome and charming and, the little she knew of him, he appeared to be an all-around swell guy. She'd been lonely, but not so much that she was ready to get involved with a man again, even one as devastatingly charismatic as Jack Campbell. Besides, legally, she was still married to Timothy.

CHAPTER 3

T hat evening, while Rose made Sarah's lunch for school tomorrow, she half-listened to her daughter's chatter as she sat on the sofa, until she said something that caught her full attention.

"Mommy, I think you should go out and have fun with Mr. Campbell. He was awful nice on the telephone."

Rose thought, *Darn you, Jack Campbell! Why did you have to call me at home with Sarah listening?*

He'd gotten Sarah's hopes up since the little scamp had always wanted a daddy. She gave Sarah an indulgent smile and pulled a pigtail the same color as her own honey-colored hair. "You just want to raise bedlam when I leave you with a babysitter."

"Babysitter?" Sarah said, rolling her eyes in a very adult-like fashion. "Mommy, I'm almost five." She sighed and gave Rose a sad look. "I just want you to be happy."

Rose frowned as she put the bagged lunch in the refrigerator, then sat down beside Sarah on the sofa. "Why do you think I'm not happy, honey? Have I said something? Am I terribly crabby when I come home from work? What is it?"

Sarah shook her head. "No, but sometimes I hear you crying."

"When?"

"In the night."

"Oh, Sarah, I'm sorry if I woke you!" Rose stroked the top of Sarah's sandy-colored curly hair.

"That's okay. I heard you say Daddy's name. You miss him a lot, don't you?"

"Every day," Rose said as she took Sarah into her arms and rocked her back and forth, though she admitted to herself silently that time passing was making it easier on her.

Sarah eventually pulled out of her mom's embrace. "So, when Mr. Campbell calls you back, tell him you want to go out. It'll be good for you."

Amazement crossed Rose's face. "When did you grow up and become so wise?"

Sarah rolled her eyes once more. "Mommy, I've always been grown up. That's what you always say."

Rose laughed. Soon they were rolling back and forth on the sofa, tickling each other.

Suddenly, Sarah jumped off the couch and as she ran down the hallway, yelled, "I almost forgot but I made my Christmas list!"

Rose groaned. *Already?* It was only September—too early to think about the holidays. Most years she felt inclined to forget the entire season—except Sarah was there to remind her.

Sarah skipped into the living room, crumpled list in hand. She unfolded it and smoothed it out on the coffee table. "There. Now don't forget to read it before bedtime tonight," she ordered.

❄

Rose spent the next morning getting her life in order. She got Sarah off to school then perused her bills, all the while thinking about Sarah's Christmas list. She had printed neatly two things on her list: a real, live kitten and, of all things, a husband for her mom. She'd addressed the letter to Santa and reminded her mother before she left for school not to forget to mail it to him soon. Meanwhile, she'd used a couple of bumble bee magnets she'd made in preschool to hold it on their refrigerator.

Sitting at her kitchen table, Sarah glanced up at the note and sighed. Most kids would have said a daddy for Christmas but not Sarah. Hers said husband for mommy.

By late morning she'd started nervously chewing on her nails when she realized if she didn't make approximately the same salary she'd been making at the bank, she'd have to find two jobs. The problem was, with the return of the soldiers she wasn't sure if she could find even one job.

She'd just finished a cup of tomato soup and a grilled-cheese sandwich when her phone rang. She crossed the kitchen and picked up the phone. "Hello?"

"Mrs. Delaney?"

Rose frowned. "Mr. Jorgenson, is that you?"

"'Course it's me! Why aren't you at work?" he growled.

"We decided yesterday I was through and that Mr. Campbell would step in right away."

"He's doing fine, but we've got a problem."

"Is that a fact?"

"Marianne Phillips's left this morning because her boyfriend returned from the war. They're getting married. She quit on me without notice. Young people have no ethics."

Good for you, Marianne! "I'm sorry," Rose said.

He groaned. "Yes, well, now there's no one to answer the phones and greet the public."

"Hire someone."

"That's what I'm trying to do. Jack said you might be interested in the job seeing as he's taken your place."

Heat traveled from Rose's face to her chest and her hand shook as she gripped the phone. "So, Mr. Campbell recommended me for the job, hmm? I've never been a receptionist before."

"He believes you're perfect for the job."

"He does, does he? After being head accountant, I'm afraid it may not be challenging enough for me."

"Maybe," he said, noncommittal at best.

"What's the rate of pay?"

Dead silence greeted her. She'd caught him off guard with the question, one a woman never dared ask when seeking a job, but waited patiently to be told the information, which usually occurred near the end of an interview.

He snapped out a figure.

"Why, I made more money four years ago working at Morley's Soda Fountain!" Rose protested.

"Yes, well, maybe that's where you should get a job then," Mr. Jorgenson snarled. "I knew I was wasting my time."

Crash! He'd slammed down the phone and Rose cringed. Placing the phone in its cradle she shrugged off his rudeness then dressed in preparation for applying for the few job offerings she'd found in the newspaper. Wearing her gray wool suit and black stiletto-heeled shoes she was confident she appeared professional. She placed a gray cloche hat sporting a jaunty feather on her head, smoothed the sides of her page boy, buttoned up her raincoat, grabbed her umbrella and headed outside.

As she stood on the street corner waiting for the streetcar, rain spattered down onto the sidewalk. She gazed pensively down at the water pooling around her feet and thought about Jorgenson's job offer. How had poor Marianne managed on such a pittance? But then she remembered the girl had lived at home with her parents.

The sound of squealing automobile wheels brought her head up. She saw the vehicle turn the corner, headed her way and groaned. It was the blue Studebaker again.

The automobile roared by, pulled a U-turn and came roaring back toward her. As the automobile drew closer, she jumped back from the curb, having learned her lesson the day before.

The driver stopped the car a few feet back from where she stood, then uncurled his long body from the driver seat as he left the automobile. Jack Campbell limped as quickly as he could toward her. Upon reaching her he ducked beneath her umbrella. She refused to raise her arm high so he could stand upright but glared at him as he half stood next to her.

His raincoat was gray, and he'd pulled his black felt fedora low on his head, his blue eyes capturing hers from beneath the brim. His appearance commanded attention, probably due to his well-above average height.

Scowling at her from his awkward, bent position he looked straight into her eyes and asked, "Why didn't you accept the job?"

She sniffed. "Do you mind? This is my umbrella."

He took the umbrella from her hand and raised it higher so he could straighten up beneath it. "Yes, well, I don't feel like getting wet. I drove over here to find out why you turned down the receptionist job."

"Bluntly put, it doesn't pay enough."

He nodded. "So I heard from Jorgenson. I tried talking him into a higher rate of pay but he wouldn't budge. I'm here to make you another job offer."

She lifted her brow, tried concentrating on his words rather than on his attractive male presence. He emanated strength and masculinity, and yet she felt his deep warmth as well. She imagined being held in his muscular arms; imagined his kisses, knowing they'd be sweet at first, then more persistent as they grew to know each other.

"Interested in hearing about it?" he asked.

"There isn't another job vacant at the moment."

"Yes, there is—a newly created one, by me. I need a secretary."

She shrugged. "So have the new receptionist do your typing. Marianne helped me on occasion."

"Jorgenson's got big plans for expanding the bank's services, especially the mortgage end of it. He's anticipating the house building market to pick up now that the men have come home from the war, which means we'll have more business coming into the bank. I need a secretary and Jorgenson agreed."

"I attended school to be an accountant, not a secretary."

He scowled. "I know, but the pay will be better than what the receptionist position pays."

"Will it be equal in pay to your position?"

Jack tugged at his collar. "Afraid not," he muttered. "Be reasonable. Don't you think it would be strange if the secretary made as much as the boss?" He quoted the wages.

"Better, but still not enough." She sighed. "I worked all morning on my household budget and know I can't make it on less pay than I'd been making as an accountant."

"I'll personally make up the difference."

Rose gasped and snatched back her umbrella. "Absolutely not!"

With a fist, he lifted her chin and stared into her eyes. In a gentle, enticing voice, he said, "I've another proposal then."

Proposal? She held onto her hat, felt and heard blood pumping through her body, her heart racing at his words, her imagination taking flight.

"I need a wife."

Rose widened her eyes, unable to believe his words. She couldn't help closing them when he moved closer and wound his arms around her waist, drawing her nearer.

"Yes, marriage would nicely solve both our problems," he whispered as he took her lips in a fervent kiss.

The kiss didn't last long—not nearly as long as she would have liked. But as soon as he lifted his lips from hers, common sense prompted Rose to pull out of his arms.

He swiped a raindrop off the tip of her nose. "Perhaps I'm premature in proposing."

"I'll say," she retorted.

"I meant what I said. I need a wife."

"What for?"

He grinned. "That's a silly question, don't you think?"

"Not at all. You speak of securing a wife with little more thought than finding a housekeeper or a cook. By the way, how many other women have you proposed to since returning from the war?"

He threw back his head and laughed as he playfully wrestled the umbrella from her once more. "No one else, Rose. We'd be good together."

"You don't love me."

He didn't dispute her comment but said in a low, smooth tone, "I could easily *learn* to love you, as you would learn to love me. And let's not deny the fact we're physically attracted to each other. That's important, you know."

Rose sighed. "I won't deny I find you attractive, but I can't marry a stranger."

"Let me ask you this then. If war was starting right now and I proposed, would you accept?"

Oh, my! Did I have the same feelings I'd had when Timothy proposed?

"The truth," he added, his blue eyes delving into hers.

She knew the answer would be 'yes', even though she didn't want to be honest and tell him so. It wasn't normal to fall in love so quickly. Love? What in the world was she thinking?

He drew her up onto her toes and lowered his head. "It's true, isn't it? You would marry me," he insisted.

She shrugged nonchalantly even though her heart was beating wildly. "Perhaps."

"I want to kiss you again."

"It won't convince me to accept your proposal. Also, I am still married, you know."

He stepped back and frowned. "No, I didn't know. Wasn't your husband killed?"

"Not sure. He's listed as missing so, technically, I am still married to Timothy."

"Legally, I guess that could prevent a problem for us then," he mused. "Let me look into that though. Now about kissing you again."

"Yes," she breathed, tilting her head back, giving into the moment, giving into his charm, ignoring the voice inside telling her she was being unfaithful to Timothy. Her hat fell to the ground as he swooped down and took her lips in a fervent kiss once more. When he released her, he squeezed her tight against his chest and rocked her in his arms.

His scent, a combination of wool, old spice, tobacco, and man, appealed to her. She sniffled and tears gathered in her eyes. Oh, life would be so much easier if she were to marry him. But she couldn't help but wonder why he'd proposed to her when they didn't know each other, nor did they love each other. But then, she'd known of marriages of convenience, where each person would bring what the other needed to the marriage, and love would grow over time.

Rose came to a decision, stepping out of his embrace. "I think we need to get to know each other much better before we indulge ourselves further."

He smiled. "You mean before we allow things to go too far between us?" She blushed at his words and he continued, "Do you *want* to get to know me? Your kiss tells me you do, but then I can be persuasive. It's not because I'm pressuring you, is it?"

"Oh," she laughed, "I believe I could get used to your pressure tactics, Jack Campbell."

His smile deepened. "I love hearing you say my name. How about dinner and a movie this Saturday night?"

"Perhaps. Call me later in the week, won't you?"

"You can count on it," he said, his voice firm.

The sky lit up and lightning struck nearby.

He nodded at his automobile. "Let's get in and out of the rain," he said.

With her head tilted back, she gasped when her hat started falling even as Jack snatched it up, took the umbrella and collapsed it, then pulled her to the Studebaker and helped her inside. He settled in behind the wheel, checked her over and laughed.

"We are soaked to the skin, even though we'd been standing beneath your umbrella. By the way, where were you going?"

"Job hunting."

He scowled. "I've offered you a job as my secretary."

"And I've already told you it doesn't pay enough." Rose sighed when the streetcar rumbled by and met his eyes. "That was the only streetcar I could take. Would you please drop me off downtown on your way back to work?"

"I can't convince you to take the job, can I? And you won't marry me. If you did you wouldn't have to worry about money."

"You're tempting me, you know."

"Of course I am."

She shook her head. "I'm not ready for that big step in my life, Jack. But, a night of dinner, music and dancing I may consider."

He sighed and placed his hands on the steering wheel. "Well, guess I can't argue with that bit of progress, can I?"

He left her off at the St. Paul Press newspaper building but claimed another kiss first, which left Rose's head reeling.

It turned out the accounting job she'd found in the paper had already been filled. She applied for accounting positions at two other businesses, but again discovered both companies had finished hiring back men who'd returned home from active duty. As she rode the streetcar home, depression settled deep inside her. She supposed she could sell her home and purchase a smaller, more modest one, but there weren't too many houses more modest than her tiny, two-bedroom house as it was.

Apartment living was expensive, and she didn't like the idea of living in one with Sarah. Children required a yard and most apartments didn't take animals, which meant she'd need to find a home for the kitten she planned on getting for Sarah for Christmas.

Once she arrived home, she changed into a casual red plaid wool skirt and sweater and perused her bills again. She tried rearranging the dates she paid them, but it didn't help. And she hadn't been living extravagantly, either. The resentment she'd been feeling toward Jack and other men who'd returned to their jobs hadn't diminished.

In most marriages, men were responsible for the bills, taking care of a wife and children, and on the income she'd been earning as an accountant. She would hold no grudge toward a married man being hired for a position ahead of her, but Jack wasn't married. He did seem to want commitment, though, and she wondered why. While Rose had no idea of Jack's age, she did know young men loved sowing wild oats before marrying. Perhaps he was older than he appeared and had sowed plenty of oats already.

Rose heard the front door open and Sarah's happy voice calling, "Mommy! How come you're home already from work?"

Luckily, her neighbor, Barb Bradford, who drove Sarah to

and home from school each day, also babysat for two hours until Rose arrived home from work. Rose willingly paid her for that care and now, while she hadn't wanted to tell her daughter she'd lost her job, which would cause her to worry, she decided she had to be honest.

Sarah ran into the kitchen and threw herself into her mother's arms.

With a hug, Rose explained, "For a while I'll be home to meet you right after school so you won't be staying next door with Mrs. Bradford."

"How come?"

"Because I lost my job, sweetheart, but I'll find a new one soon."

Worry settled over Sarah's small face. "Are we poor now?"

Rose laughed. "No, silly! I receive a small survivor's pension from the military so no, we won't starve."

"Don't they need you at the bank anymore?"

"You know how I told you when the war ended the soldiers would need their jobs back? Well, the war's ended and Mr. Campbell has taken his job back."

"Oh." Sarah frowned. "Won't he share the job with you?"

Oh, to be so young and innocent. "Honey, no, he can't. He has to earn a living, too."

"He got kids?"

Rose assumed he didn't since he wasn't married, yet one never knew. Of course, she couldn't tell Sarah that!

"No."

Indignantly, Sarah said, "Did you tell him you got me?"

"I did. Now don't worry. I'll find another job. We'll do fine."

CHAPTER 4

"Ahhh!" The scream tore through Jack's apartment, waking him from a sound sleep early Friday morning. As he sat up in his bed, heart racing, hands shaking, he searched his bedroom for an intruder.

All was quiet. It was then Jack realized he'd had another dream—another nightmare that had ripped him from his peaceful slumber. Groaning, he flopped back on the bed and covered his eyes with his forearm, gained control of his erratic breathing, thankful he couldn't recall much of the nightmare. Would they ever stop, he wondered? Or, would he carry war horrors for the rest of his life? He prayed not.

As he rested, pleasant thoughts of Rose slipped into his mind. His lips lifted into a smile and he chuckled, thinking about the beautiful woman he'd just met. Then his smile slipped as guilt permeated his conscience. He'd taken away her livelihood with his return. He wasn't happy about it, but then, he needed the job if he had any hope of earning money to help him start up his own business. His inheritance from his grandmother would stay in the bank, per the marriage requirement.

He couldn't deny his attraction for Rose, but understood it

wasn't love he was feeling—yet. But he planned on getting real close to her, hoping to convince her there were worse things in life than a marriage of convenience. Their love for each other would grow with time.

By Friday night Rose had cold feet about her Saturday night date with Jack. The man was too attractive for his own good, and for her peace of mind.

It didn't help she'd had an awful week and ended up with not a single job interview. Once again, the old resentment she'd felt earlier toward the Jack reappeared. If she didn't find a decent paying accounting job by the end of next week, she might have to eat crow and give into Jack's idea about being his secretary, assuming he hadn't hired someone else for the position.

She'd learned about a newly formed support group for war widows that met at the local Lutheran church. She didn't know if she was a widow since Timothy's body hadn't been found, still, she'd joined, hoping to seek information which could help her in her job prospects. This evening was the first meeting.

Three hours later, as she left the meeting, she was even more depressed. Most of the women who'd attended were actively seeking only one thing; getting married again! They didn't care about securing another job and had been glad to leave behind the ones they'd worked during the war years.

Rose had to wonder at herself; was she abnormal for enjoying working and not staying home? But then, she thought if she'd had the luxury, and had more children, besides, she likely would enjoy being home. Unfortunately, it had never been an option for her, unless she remarried.

The idea was tempting, and she wasn't growing any

younger. The thought of having another baby was enticing. Perhaps she should reconsider Jack's offer.

She'd just put Sarah to bed and had slipped into her nightgown when the phone rang. As she tore into the kitchen, she wished she'd had a telephone installed in her bedroom. But then, it wasn't often she had calls at nine o'clock at night.

"Hello?"

"Hi Rose. It's Jack."

She smiled and leaned against the kitchen counter. "Hi, how are you?"

"Great. How was the job hunting? Find something yet?"

She sighed. "Unfortunately, no."

"You haven't given it enough time, though I have to admit with the guys taking back their jobs, it might not be easy either."

"I have all the time in the world to pursue a new job, but there just aren't many available, well-paying positions. Sure, there are plenty of jobs but none that pay as well as the accounting position which you now occupy."

"Is that resentment I hear in your voice?"

She snapped, "You don't know me well enough to be judgmental, Jack Campbell!"

"Hey, hey, calm down now—"

"You're telling me I should calm down when you've only yourself to consider. I have a daughter, a mortgage, and utility bills to pay, and groceries to purchase."

"Maybe you need to learn how to manage your money better, sweetheart."

Rose trembled in fury at his condescending remark, unable to believe his audacity. She stumbled over her words but managed to spit them out. "Need I remind you I'm an accountant? I've been caring for my daughter for years, without a man's support."

He sighed. "Yes, I know you're an accountant, and from

all I've seen, a darned good one. Ignore my last remark, it was uncalled for."

"All right," she said, her voice still shaking.

"I didn't call to argue with you, you know."

"Could have fooled me."

He laughed. "I called to find out what movie you want to see tomorrow night. I've already chosen a place to have dinner."

"Oh! Well, I haven't seen a movie in years and have no idea what's showing. You decide."

"I love a woman who makes me feel like a man by leaving me to make the decisions," he said softly.

His comment gave her pause. Oh, yes, he was all man, all right.

"We've got dinner reservations for five-thirty. I know it's early, but I don't want us to rush. It will also allow us enough time to get to the theater. Okay?"

"Sure. See you tomorrow," she whispered, then quickly hung up. She frowned out the kitchen window, wondering where her resolve had gone. She'd planned on calling off the date but hadn't managed to maneuver their conversation in that direction. He was a persuasive man. She warned herself to be on her guard with him at all times.

Rose spent most of Saturday catching up on housework and washing clothes.

Sarah had been invited to a friend's birthday party for the afternoon, which left Rose time to not only finish her cleaning but to take a luxurious, relaxing bubble bath before her date.

After her skin had wrinkled from sitting in the steamy bubble-bath, she reluctantly pulled the plug. Then she rummaged through her closet until she found what she believed was the perfect dress for dinner and a movie.

It was a black, lightweight wool sheath with a heart-shaped neckline, which showed her long neck to perfection. The sleeves were elbow-length and snug, the dress itself fit her quite tightly, as did most of the fashions made during the war. After all, fabric and time spent on sewing went into making uniforms for the soldiers.

Styles had changed in the last year, though. With the war's end, skirts were fuller and fashioned with much more fabric. She hadn't been able to afford new dresses, but she knew the sheath was attractive on her. She wore a black lacy brassiere beneath it, and a matching black lace panty and garter belt with her last pair of silk stockings. She prayed the stockings with runs she'd sent to Kennington's for repair would be returned to her soon.

She stepped into a pair of black three-inch pumps with open toes just as Sarah arrived home from her party. After feeding her a supper of macaroni and cheese, garden peas, and toast, the doorbell rang.

Sixteen-year-old Sue Ellen Pearson, Sarah's favorite baby-sitter, had arrived with her 'bag of tricks'. Rose was impressed with the girl's efforts and appreciated the attention she gave Sarah.

Rose was putting on the finishing touches of her makeup, including a lush new red lipstick she'd splurged on called carnation red when the doorbell rang. Quickly, she clipped on a pair of pearl earrings and matching choker-style necklace, then rushed down the hallway to meet her date.

She arrived in the front hallway in time to see Sarah take Jack's hand and lead him into the living room. He followed, smiling down at her until he suddenly looked up and directly into Rose's eyes as she stood in the arched doorway leading into the living room.

"Oh, Mommy!" Sarah said, "I didn't think you were ready. I want to show Mr. Campbell some magic tricks Sue Ellen taught me."

"Okay, honey," Rose said. "If Mr. Campbell wants to."

Jack glanced down at his gold watch. "We've got about ten minutes before we need to leave."

Rose nodded, her face heating up when she saw how his eyes lingered on her, sweeping over her body.

She pulled her raincoat from the closet, found her black cloth gloves and matching hat with a small veil and strolled into the living room. Jack's larger than life presence seemed to dwarf the living room. It was tiny, yet never had it felt this small. He sat on a too-small barrel-backed stuffed chair as her daughter spread cards out across the coffee table, asking him to choose two cards.

After Sarah completed the trick he laughed aloud and complimented her on her expertise. As Rose watched him with her daughter, she decided he seemed to be a natural with kids. Soon they left the house, and he kept her arm tucked through his while they walked to his automobile.

He opened the passenger door. "That's some kid you've got there, Rose."

Rose laughed. "She sure is. I'm not sure what I'd do without her. She's wonderful company and, as you've noticed, has a great sense of humor."

"And she's smart, too," he noted. "I could tell just from how well she played out those card tricks." He grinned. "She takes after you, you know. You're lucky to have her."

"Yes, I am," Rose said.

He settled her inside the Studebaker. Once he sank into the driver seat, he didn't start the engine. Instead, he said, "I've something for you." He reached over the back seat, his arm brushing her shoulder.

She sucked in her breath, closed her eyes as the heady sensation and his scent seeped into her senses.

Jack pulled a red gift-wrapped box over the seat and handed it to her.

"Oh, Jack. You shouldn't have!" she exclaimed, even as

she tore into the paper and tried to remember when she'd last received a gift from a man. Quite a while ago, she mused, thinking this courting business wasn't too bad, after all.

Inside the box she found thirty chocolate covered cherries in three neat rows. Her mouth watered. Chocolates had been at a premium for so long. She gave him a pleading look.

He chuckled. "Go ahead and have a couple. They shouldn't spoil your dinner. And I'd like you to wear this."

Her eyes misted with tears when he gently lifted an orchid wrist corsage from a gold box in his lap.

As he slipped it over her wrist he said, "That's why I kept the Studebaker running; didn't want the flowers to die because of the cold before you had a chance to enjoy them."

Rose was overwhelmed by his thoughtfulness. Timothy hadn't spent much time courting her. She'd never received flowers from him or candy, but he had given her the love of her life, their precious daughter. But then, Timothy had been an inexperienced young man while Jack was a sophisticated man in his prime.

She wiped her cheek with her gloved hand, catching a tear. Jack's hand replaced hers and he settled it on her cheek. She glanced up quickly, met the concerned look in his eyes.

"What's wrong? I didn't mean to make you cry. What did I do?"

"Everything!" she choked out, turning to stare blindly out the window as more tears clouded her vision.

"Hey," he said softly.

When he placed an arm around her shoulder, she turned to him and buried her face against his topcoat. Her tears fell in earnest then.

"Shush sweetheart, it's all right. If you don't like the flowers I'll understand. Here," he said as he moved back from her. He touched her wrist, started pulling off the corsage when she clamped her hand down on his.

"No! I love the flowers, and the candy, and—"

"And?" he said.

She gulped. "And our date, which we haven't really had yet. Okay? I'm just not used to all of the courtly attention," she muttered in embarrassment.

After a long moment's silence, she heard him clear his throat then say, "I like the hat. Does the veil come down across your eyes?"

She frowned. "Huh? What does my hat have to do with what we are talking about?"

He grinned. "Not a thing, but you're not crying anymore."

Rose had never felt more like pulling out her hair, or his.

Jack looked at her curiously. "Didn't your husband court you before you married?"

"Remember when you asked if I'd marry you if we were just entering the war and I said I likely would?"

He nodded and she continued, "Well, that's what happened with me and Timothy, which is the reason why he never really courted me. He didn't have the time. We were married, then he left the next day for active duty. But if he'd had the time, I don't think he could have topped you in the courting department. We were both pretty young when we married, and he'd never dated another girl."

With a sheepish smile on his face, Jack said, "And I'll bet you'd never dated another guy before your husband, had you?"

"No."

He sighed. "I know you think I'm some kind of Casanova, but I'm not. I've only been with a few girls—seriously."

"Truly?"

"Yes." He looked at his watch. "We've got to get going otherwise we'll lose our dinner reservation."

During the fifteen-minute drive to the restaurant Rose surreptitiously studied the man beside her. He was a tall, handsome man who seemed oblivious to his good looks and charm. And he had a sharp mind, too. She recalled going over some complicated records over the phone a few times during the past week and how quickly he'd understood her explanations.

He sort of reminded her of the comic book hero, Dick Tracy, with his fedora slanted low and over one eye, his strong, chiseled jaw, and piercing blue eyes, though his hair was lighter.

Jack took her to DePaola's, a fine Italian restaurant with a northern Italian cuisine menu. After eating lasagna accompanied by a bottle of Chianti, Rose placed her hand over her glass when Jack went to fill it for the third time.

"Two's my limit, unless you plan on carrying me to the car."

He kissed her hand, then looked up into her eyes. "Or I could take you home with me and have my wicked way with you."

CHAPTER 5

R ose gasped, "Perish the thought, you devilish man!"
Jack grinned and sank back in his chair. He reached
into his pocket and pulled out a package of cigarettes. "Do
you mind?"

She shook her head but replied, "No, but I hate the
smell."

"No problem. Trying to quit anyway," he said as
repocketed the package. "I'm just fooling around, Rose. I
respect you and would never do anything you wouldn't want."

Which was a big problem for Rose because right about
now she wanted him a lot.

"We'll miss the start of the movie if you don't finish
soon," he added.

"Oh, no!" She set down her fork and snatched up her
purse, ready to rise from their table when he covered her
hand.

"Finish your meal. I've a better idea."

"You have?"

"Yes. See the dance floor over there?"

She followed his nod, noted the shiny wooden floor across
the room and nodded.

"How about instead of a show we dance the night away."

"What about your leg? I mean, I don't mind just listening to the band play, if you'd rather."

His eyes glittered with mischief as he stood, picked up his chair and moved it beside hers. He sank down and said, "I'd much rather spend the time dancing, no need to worry. According to my doctor I should be able to handle the slow dances. Do you mind holding up an injured soldier for a while?"

Rose smiled gently, patted his hand. "I'd be honored to dance with you, Captain."

Unfortunately, the first dance music the band played was too fast for Jack. Another man arrived at their table and requested a dance with Rose. Jack wanted to punch the guy in the nose but graciously said, instead, it was Rose's decision.

He saw her bite her lower lip, indecision on her face, so he gave her an encouraging nod. He admitted he was disappointed when she went with the guy and proceeded to dance two dances in quick succession. Another one started playing and he lost sight of her on the floor. Disappointment set in just as a set of arms wound around his neck from behind, and a cheek was pressed gently against his.

"Did you miss me, Captain Jack?" Rose's sweet voice asked.

"Captain Jack?" he growled over the music and pulled her around to his front and settled her on his lap.

The movement surprised her, and she tried to stand but he held her in place. "The Captain wants you to stay and keep him company for a while." She squirmed but he clamped his hand around her waist. "Be still."

"Someone will see us!" she protested.

"No one can see us in this dark corner. I want you to wait here with me until they play a slow dance."

❄

Rose relaxed and heaved a deep sigh when Jack reached up and massaged her neck and back. He was surprised to feel her sharp protruding bones and frowned. She was too thin and needed some fattening up. He knew she watched every cent, and now, with no job, she would be even more careful. He also knew she'd suffer starvation so that her daughter would have enough to eat.

He made the decision that she must accept his offer to be his secretary. Besides, he truly did need one, but only Rose would do for the position. Sweet Rose, lovely Rose, the Rose of his heart. *He loved her.* Oh-oh, where'd that thought come from, he mused? But after another moment's thought, he was forced to face reality; he'd found the woman for him, and there were only two small problems he could see; she enjoyed working when he didn't want a working wife. And, she seemed content with her single status in life with just her daughter.

He'd had to use all his wits to convince her to go out on this date with him, and guessed she'd probably give him difficulty about future ones. But he'd made his plans to court her gently, sweetly and, once she became his secretary and they spent more time together, she'd see how much she meant to him. Eventually, she'd fall in love with him and would accept his proposal. He'd have to bide his time, though, and not ask her too soon. He gave himself a reminder to check with the army about her missing husband.

Finally, the band started playing the haunting, romantic song, *Laura,* and he rose and helped her to her feet. He pulled her along behind him, his hand clasped tightly around hers. Her hand was small, trusting, too, he noticed. He gulped as feelings he'd never felt before tore through his heart. And then, when he faced her and pulled her into his arms, he knew for certain this woman would become his wife, mother of his children, if God willed it, and no other woman would do.

He had no problem dancing the slow dances. It helped she was an excellent dancer and followed him easily. She was so small in his arms and, if she hadn't been wearing the high-heeled shoes, he would have had to hunch down in order to hold her comfortably. But then he smiled as he danced with her, her soft hair brushing against his chin. If she'd worn shorter shoes, he would have had a good enough excuse to sweep her off her feet and into his arms.

As though she'd read his mind, she moved back from him, grimacing. "My feet are killing me. I'd like to rest a bit if you don't mind. Besides, your ankle must be causing you pain, too, isn't it?"

"Not a bit," he said, "but I've an idea."

He pulled her from the floor and into a curtained alcove, a perfect lover's trysting place, he thought. But he wouldn't make love to her—not until their wedding night, for he respected her too much. But he also didn't want to stop dancing with her but knew she couldn't continue with her sore feet.

"Jack, what are we doing in here?"

"Take off your shoes," he ordered.

She stared at him. "Why, for heaven's sake?"

"You said your feet were sore."

"They are! But I can't remove them until I get home."

"Remove them here because I'm not ready to stop dancing."

He gave her an innocent smile and Rose narrowed her eyes on him. "Just what do you have in mind, Captain Jack?"

"This," he growled, and he swung her up into his arms. Then he pulled off her shoes and tossed them onto a narrow velvet bench curved in a U-shape around the alcove. He swayed with her in his arms, one arm around her back, the other beneath her thighs as he held her close.

Satisfaction soared through him when her surprise disappeared and she settled her head against his shoulder, her arms went around his neck. He held her in his arms, danced two dances this way, and never wanted to stop.

Finally, he released her, and she danced with him, her feet settled on the top of his shoes for several more dances.

Finally, she lifted her head. "We'd better leave. The babysitter has to be home by eleven and it's already half past ten."

He released her legs and watched her as she bent down and found her shoes, then held his arm as she shoved her feet inside them. She groaned.

He chuckled. "Want me to carry you out of here?"

Rose gasped, "You can't! Your leg…"

"You don't think I can?" he inserted. "You know, taking you home is the furthest thing from my mind at the moment. But, if you insist, don't let it be said I caused your poor feet any more pain."

He bent to her, but she hopped back. "You wouldn't dare!" She started to turn away when he swept her off her feet and into his arms once more.

"Jack!" she gasped just as he yanked back the velvet curtain.

He stared at her, eyes flashing with humor. "Never dare a soldier, sweetheart."

Jack noted only a small crowd of people remained, and they applauded when he limped out of the restaurant and toward the lobby with his delightful burden protesting fervently in his arms. He couldn't let her go yet. He never wanted to let her go.

After the first few protests and squirming, she settled down as he made his way to the coat check. She raised her head and looked at him, anticipating his setting her on her feet, but he didn't. He sat down on a vacant chair, settled her on his lap and assisted her with her coat. As soon as she'd stuffed her arms inside, he settled his coat over her.

"Now you'll be doubly warm," he insisted, grinning into

her flushed face and blue eyes sparking with fury. He enjoyed seeing her angry. She appeared much like a thwarted kitten. Plain and simple, she was adorable.

But he grew uncomfortable with her silence on the drive home, even though he'd tried making pleasant conversation. Could she be that angry with him she wouldn't speak to him again? She shouldn't be embarrassed. The people at the restaurant likely thought they were married, anyway, and out on the town for an anniversary or some other special occasion.

Jack pulled up to her house and anticipated Rose's quick move, thwarting her attempt to leave the car by stretching across her and jamming his hand on the door handle.

She'd pulled the veil over her face. In the darkness, he had difficulty making out her features. As he leaned over her, staring hard into her face, he said, "What's got your goat, Rose?"

"Nothing," she softly replied. "I really do need to get inside."

"Not until you tell me what's wrong? Did I embarrass you back there?"

She shoved her veil back and glared at him. "What do you think?"

He sighed, then turned sideways in the seat. He laid his arm along the back of the seat behind her and stared at her. He hadn't thought her a prude, but she certainly was behaving like one. But then it hit him; there was a possibility she was angry because she was more than a bit attracted to him. Up until they were ready to leave, she'd seemed delighted to be dancing, held in his arms. She'd accepted his few chaste kisses along her temple. She was fighting her attraction for him, why, he wasn't certain. But he was ready and armed, ready to pursue her with an arsenal of charm she wouldn't be able to resist for long.

"What do I think?" he asked casually. "I think I want to kiss you, and I think you want me to kiss you, too."

He saw her jaw tighten and her eyes narrow.

"Of all the—"

"Nerve? Right. Now be honest with yourself. You want the same, but you're fighting me. For some reason, you don't want to become involved with me. I intend to find out why because I plan on making you my wife, Rose, sooner or later."

She bit her lip and stared down at her hands. After a long moment she leaned over, placed her palm against his heart and kissed him on the cheek. He started winding an arm around her waist when she pulled back from him and opened her door. "Good-Night, Captain Jack."

Jack watched her run up the sidewalk leading to her house. How long he stayed he couldn't tell, but it was long enough for him to come up with another plan of attack.

Shortly after Jack left, Sue Ellen's ride showed up. After the teenager left, Rose sighed and sank down in a chair at the kitchen table. Handling Jack Campbell was proving to be a problem. The man was too intuitive, which was surprising due to the fact she'd never met a man with good instincts before. Women seemed to possess that characteristic more than men, at least in her experience.

She hadn't truly been angry with his caveman tactics but had been disturbed by her own feelings, ones she thought she'd buried long ago. He was attractive, gentle, kind and sweet. And she was falling head over heels for him.

Rose knew he was more than a little attracted to her. So, why wasn't she happy about it? Her conscience chided her. *You know exactly why!* Thoughts of Timothy entered her mind then. Losing your heart to a man—falling in love will only bring heartache, in the end.

Nothing lasted forever.

CHAPTER 6

October 1946

"When are you going to come to your senses, Jack?"

Jack lounged on the sofa in his parents' spacious living room, his eyes on his father who paced the floor directly in Jack's line of vision.

When Jack didn't reply, his tall, gray-haired father glared at him. "Well?"

Having lived through several of these uncomfortable, tension-fraught moments, Jack took his father's fury in stride. "I believe my idea of sense and yours are two different things, Father."

"You can say that again!" John Campbell, Sr. growled. "Enlisting in the U.S. Army and leaving home the way you did, why, it wasn't necessary."

"I'm no coward. I had strong feelings about the war and needed to do my part."

"Your part?" the older man scoffed. "The damned war's left you a cripple!"

"Now, John, remember your blood pressure," said Jack's

mother, Jeanne, as she entered the living room, coffee tray in hand.

Jack rose quickly from the sofa and eased the tray from his mother's hands with a grin. He caught the twinkle in her eyes, though she kept her expression serious as she sat down in a chair across from him.

John harrumphed. "Well, you're home now, and that's all that matters. Think over my offer some more before you come to a final decision." He stalked from the living room.

Jack's gaze followed him until he disappeared out the door, then he sank back on the sofa, relief settling over him. Jack met his mother's eyes. "Well, now, that wasn't so bad, was it?"

She smiled sadly. "Won't you reconsider his offer, dear? You are, after all, his only child." She leaned over the coffee table and poured them each a cup of coffee and handed one to Jack.

"No," Jack replied, "I can't, Mother. I refuse to live the life he's lived for years."

"But aren't you proud of the company he's built? And you know, he did it all for you."

Scowling, now, Jack replied, "Oh, come on, he did it for himself, not for me, or for you. You're having delusions about him and his love for us, you know. You've always made excuses for his behavior, but there's no excuse for a husband and father leaving wife and family behind for months at a time, unless there's a war on. No, I won't take over the steel company."

"Then, what will you do? You can't stay at that banking job forever, you know."

"I've no intention in staying at LaSalle, but I've goals for my future that I think you might be interested in hearing about." He went on to tell her about his future company and building homes. He saw her delight, especially when he mentioned his plans to marry Rose Delaney.

"Do you love her?"

Her question triggered an immediate reaction from him, and, in a firm voice, he replied, "Yes. I've thought about this over the past two weeks—tried telling myself it was much too soon to fall in love with a woman I'd just met, but it's true. I have to face my feelings that I do, indeed, love her."

After their dinner-dance date, Jack had had difficulty convincing Rose to see him again. She was running, fast and hard, from any involvement, but he was tenacious about pursuing his own goals. And Rose had definitely become a goal for him. He'd asked himself if he would have pursued her with such fervency if she'd made it easier on him and had easily, willingly, accepted his requests to see her. After just a moment's thought he realized his feelings would have been the same; he was in love with the shy, hard-to-get dame, but he meant to make her his bride, soon.

Over the past month he'd called her several times, stopped by her house on occasion and took her and her daughter to lunch, but she'd resisted accepting another official date, still he was confident he'd wear her down eventually.

"You know, of course, your father will be difficult about this since Rose doesn't travel in our circle of society."

"That's his loss, Mother. Do you mind?"

She smiled. "Not at all."

"Why is Father so persistent about me following in his footsteps, do you think?"

"You know the answer! He came from nothing and made something out of his life. He's a fighter, just like you. He founded a dynasty and married a high-society girl." She gave him a derisive smile, and added, "Who also happened to come with a nice inheritance. I admit at first I thought he'd wanted to marry me for that reason alone but found with the passing of time that wasn't the case at all. Your father's always had difficulty showing his love, but he does love us, never doubt that."

"You can say that again," Jack retorted. "I can't recall when he showed any physical signs of love for me, or for you, for that matter."

"Your father tends to reciprocate, but not initiate. Haven't you noticed how I usually kiss and hug him first then he responds?"

Jack felt heat seep into his cheeks as he thought over her words, realizing she was right. "Yes, I have noticed, but not until you just called my attention to it." He frowned. "Why is that, do you think?"

"He had an awful relationship with his parents because nothing he did satisfied them. I believe he's spent his entire life trying to prove, first to them, them to us, that he was good enough."

"You mean because he's been able to provide the physical things in life for his family?"

She nodded.

Jack shook his head, a wry expression on his face. "I just wished he'd spent less time worrying about giving us luxuries and more time attending my ball games and band concerts."

"I know, but he was a driven man, still is in some ways, as are you."

He tightened his jaw. "What are you saying? That I'm like him?" he growled.

She laughed, rose from her chair and sank down on the sofa beside him. She leaned her head on his shoulder and said, "More than you think." She raised her head and swiped a lock of hair back off his forehead. "Just don't lose sight of the people you love in life, especially your wife. Life passes so quickly."

"I don't plan on following in Father's footsteps, you can count on it."

❄

"I've no choice but to accept his offer, Linda," Rose said into the phone. She lounged on her bed the classified job ads scattered across her chenille bedspread.

"Just temporarily, you mean, until something better appears. Right?" her friend replied.

"Absolutely," Rose said and circled another ad. "I'm attracted to him, unfortunately. That's not a good thing."

"There's nothing wrong with a girl having fun on her job."

Rose caught the laughter in her friend's voice. "You should talk! How about you?"

Linda chuckled. "Don't worry about me, kiddo. My time will come."

Linda Warner was Rose's best friend, even though distance separated them, and they saw each other only during the Christmas season. They'd been childhood friends but, for the past ten years, Linda had lived in New York, pursuing a career as a trial lawyer. She'd done well for herself, but she hadn't found the man with whom to share her dreams.

She felt bad for Linda, especially since Rose had found happiness, even if it had only been for a fleeting moment. And, Timothy had blessed her with her sweet daughter.

Rose had been astonished when she'd first called Linda this evening and learned of her friend's plans to have a baby, even though she wasn't married. Rose adamantly tried talking Linda out of these plans, telling her she'd be ostracized for life, and it could possibly hurt her career.

Linda agreed with the first but not the last and said she'd made up her mind. She was now on the hunt for the perfect daddy donor; one who'd be willing to impregnate her without marriage; she wanted a baby, not a husband.

After Rose hung up, she noted the time at three o'clock, then, before she lost her nerve, she dialed LaSalle Bank. She didn't recognize the woman's voice who answered her call.

Must be the new receptionist, she mused, even as the woman politely put her on hold to get Jack.

She jumped, startled by Jack's impatient voice. "Hello?" he barked.

"Uh, Jack? Not a good time for you?"

"Rose? Of course it's a good time! How have you been?"

"Fine, thanks, and you?"

"Oh, just peachy keen," he drawled. "Find a job yet?"

She sighed. "No, which is the reason I'm calling. You still need a secretary?"

"Yes!" he shouted. "When can you start?"

"Whenever you want."

"Monday would be great. Excuse me a minute."

Rose heard mumbling and laughter in the background. She heard Jack's eager sounding voice and Mr. Jorgenson's gruff response. Obviously, Jack had been telling Mr. Jorgenson she was returning to work.

"Rose? What time do you want to start Monday?"

"I think the question is what time would you like me there?" she said dryly.

"Jorgenson, er, well," he said, stumbling over his words.

She frowned. *What was wrong with the man?* "Jack?"

"I'm here. Jorgenson wants to know if you can arrive by 7:30 a.m."

Rose knew precisely why Jorgenson wanted her to arrive early. "Sorry, not possible since I can't leave the house before Sarah leaves for school. Tell Mr. Jorgenson he can wait until 8:30 for me to arrive, or he can make his own coffee."

Jack's rumbling laughter made Rose smile. She loved his laugh; rich, booming, genuine. Yes, there was a definite genuineness to Jack, and she found herself growing more and more attracted to him with each passing day. But then, after a moment, she decided perhaps it was because she hadn't seen him much since their one and only date.

"Come when you can, Rose. I look forward to working

with you. Now I'll have more than work to look forward to each day."

Rose scowled when she heard him disconnect, then hung up her phone. He hadn't given up pursuing her. In a way, she was delighted and flattered he was still interested in her. She admitted *he* interested her but then sanity intruded once more; she had a child to support and a mortgage, and not enough time in the day to allow a man into her life on a permanent basis.

Her lips turned up into a smile as she thought how Jack would react to the fact that she didn't date men with whom she worked. But then, with the little she knew of him, she wouldn't put it past him to fire her because of it.

Rose stood in her next-door neighbor, Barb's driveway and waved at Sarah leaving for school. She'd bundled her crabby daughter into her woolen winter jacket, made her wear long underwear, a cap and mittens as the first snowfall had arrived overnight. Sarah didn't mind dressing for the weather, if she could have stayed home to play in the snow, but it was Monday and a school day, and Rose's first day on the job as Jack's secretary.

As she turned to walk back to her house, she wound her hands around her waist, shivering in her navy double-breasted serge coat. A horn honked and she swiveled around to see Jack drive up in his Studebaker.

"Rose! You ready?"

Scowling, Rose moved to the car, peered into the window he'd cranked open. "What are you doing here?"

"Picking you up for work."

"In fifteen minutes I'm walking to meet the streetcar."

Jack grinned. "No need for you to take it, sweetheart. I

drive within a few blocks of your house every day so it isn't out of my way to give you a ride."

Rose shook her head. "I don't think it's a good idea for us to start that habit."

He ignored her response. "Get in, please." His voice was gentle but firm. Rose opened her mouth to protest when he added, threatening, "You don't want me to come after you."

Shivering at his cool tone, and at the intent expression on his face, she rolled her eyes. Then she started tapping her booted foot impatiently on the snow-covered sidewalk, tried thinking of something to say to put him in his place when she decided she was lying to herself about not wanting a ride.

Of course it was the sensible thing to do. Besides, from Jack's expression she knew he wasn't going to allow her to step foot on a streetcar today. But she also didn't want to lead him on to thinking there was hope for a relationship between them, either.

In the last week she'd made up her mind not to become involved with him personally, including abiding by her own rule to never date men from work. Then she thought of how she'd given her whole heart and being to her husband, but she'd felt cheated by his leaving her for the military, leaving her to fend for herself and her daughter. She'd learned to care for Sarah and, in the process, had learned to not depend on a man for support.

She peered at Jack, saw the unrelenting expression and said, "I have to lock up the house and fetch my purse. I'll be right back." She swiveled on her heel and strode up the sidewalk toward her house. She returned shortly with her purse and a brown lunch bag. She slid into the passenger seat and faced forward, unable to meet his eyes.

"What's that?"

Rose glanced at him, noticed him staring at her brown bag.

"My lunch."

He put the car in gear. "Tuck it away for another day. You're having lunch with me."

"Well, I never—"

"—had lunch with me? No, not yet, but you will. Give me a chance—give *us* a chance. Besides, it's only lunch. You know I'd never harm you."

"I know," she sighed. "But, I'd better mention this to you now rather than later."

He made a right hand turn then glanced at her. "What?"

"I don't date men from work."

He gave her a confident, cocky smile. "I aim to change your mind."

CHAPTER 7

O ver the next month, Rose resisted Jack's persistent overtures to court her by maintaining a strictly business relationship. But Jack knew he was wearing her down whenever he happened to look her way, especially when she sat across from him as he dictated letters to her. He'd look over to find her eyes on him, with nary a word of dictation written in her steno book.

And it seemed the more formally she treated him, the more he wanted her. *Wasn't that the way of it?* he mused, chagrinned. He pursued her with a dogged determination with the hopes of winning her over.

First he'd sent her gold-foiled boxes of chocolates, then several pairs of finely-seamed silk stockings—that particular gift earned him a kiss. But, in the end, it was the flowers that had won him her heart.

On this cold crisp, early December morning, on his way to meeting his mother for lunch, he stopped by a local florist and ordered a dozen long-stemmed red roses to be delivered to Rose at the office.

After returning to the office, he found Rose standing behind her desk, smelling the huge bouquet of roses that she'd apparently removed from its box and had been arranged in a tall crystal vase. He stood there a moment taking pleasure in just watching her, then closed the door and leaned against it. With the closing of the door she raised her eyes to his.

Jack's heart clenched when he saw tears flooded them. His gaze followed her small hand as she raised it and smoothed her light brown, shoulder length tresses, a habit of hers he'd noticed on several occasions.

"They...they're beautiful, Jack. You shouldn't have done it."

Her voice broke and Jack frowned. "You just told me you like them, but in the same breath say I shouldn't have purchased them? And why are you so sad if you love them so much?" He rolled his eyes and murmured, "Will I ever understand dames?"

She swiped the tears from the corners of her eyes and cheeks and gave him a brilliant smile. "Scram, boss, we've work to do."

He laughed, saluted her and strode into his office. Once he settled in his seat he reached for the telephone and buzzed her.

Rose immediately picked up and said, "No, you can't have the flowers back, and yes, I'll have lunch with you tomorrow."

Satisfaction soared through him. "Thought you might see things my way."

For the next two weeks, Jack escorted Rose to lunch every day. They'd just left the Four Corners Deli when Rose made her first complaint in all of that time.

"I stepped on my scale today and forced myself not to scream."

Jack raised his brow. "Oh-oh, think I can see where this is headed."

She nodded. "We can't continue like this, eating out every day," she said, a gentle smile on her lips.

He patted her hand which he'd tucked under his arm as they strolled back to the bank. "You're absolutely right."

She gave him a suspicious look. "I am?"

"Yes, we've just about exhausted all of the downtown places to eat, so I propose I take you out to dinner, instead."

Rose shook her head and sighed. "I'm afraid that won't do at all. Remember? I don't date fellow workers, most especially my boss."

"I've a remedy for that."

"You do?" she asked in surprise.

"I'll have to fire you."

She stumbled in her high heels and would have fallen flat on her face if Jack hadn't still held her hand.

"Hey, hey! You alright, sweetheart?" he said.

Rose's cheeks heated when she caught the curious looks of passersby. She yanked her arm away. "You don't mean that."

Jack's smile slipped as he stared into her eyes. She saw his nostrils flare, and something about his intent look warned her she wouldn't like his reply.

"I mean every word. If you aren't working for me then you'd have no more excuses."

"But—"

"Answer me truthfully," he interrupted, "you're attracted to me. Why are you fighting it?" He tugged on her arm and they started walking again.

Rose bit her lip, curled her arms protectively across her stomach and looked across the street at the park filled with people eating their bag lunches. She finally turned back to him and said, "If you meant you wanted nothing but a date, a bit of fun and companionship, and didn't court me with marriage on your mind, I might accept."

❆

Go easy on her, pal. No pressure! Jack kept his expression passive even though he felt like bellowing his anger and punching the wall.

He stilled his rampaging heartbeat, continued staring down at her upturned pretty face. "Agreed," he finally said.

Her eyes widened. "You do? I mean, you won't speak to me about marriage? You'll be satisfied with dating, no strings attached?"

Jack shrugged nonchalantly, even though fury tore through him. When he'd been a youth, he'd had difficulty managing his anger. Unfortunately, he'd taken after his father in that respect. Nearly four years in the service had cured him of his tendency to expect everything to immediately come his way and easily. He'd waited in lines for meals during basic training and, later, in combat drills. Learning patience was the most important thing the service had done for him, and he found himself using those skills now.

"You're calling the shots, sweetheart," he drawled, a grin on his lips. His grin widened at her surprised expression. "What? You don't believe me?"

She smiled. "Oh, I believe you, but you're so mercurial that you confuse me!" Her smile slipped then as she added, "But truthfully, you mustn't get too serious. I think I owe you more of an explanation. I gave my heart and soul—everything I had to give to Timothy. When he was gone, I hurt inside for so long, so badly, I didn't know if I'd ever heal again. Do you understand what I'm saying?"

It took him a moment to reply as sadness filled his soul; sadness for her losing her husband; sadness for himself and his severed relationship with Veronica Miller.

Maybe she was right to be cautious. It would be wise of him to follow suit, temporarily, but then he thought about Grandmother's money and knew he hadn't much choice; one way or another, he had to marry sometime in order to secure his inheritance.

"You must have loved your husband very much if you've sworn off forming any further attachments. At least, that's what I think you're saying."

She nodded. "Perhaps I'm still in the healing stages, still grieving somewhat, but I want you to know I may never heal completely. I may never want to marry again. I know you want marriage in your future, so I just don't want you to build up your hopes thinking you'll change my mind."

They'd reached the bank. He opened the door for her and escorted her inside. "We'll take things slow, for now, okay?" he said. "Let's just enjoy each other's company. I'll try and not get too serious, as you say."

They entered the elevator and Rose said thoughtfully, "Perhaps I'm having trouble with closure of my marriage, and not wanting to make a commitment to anyone, because Timothy is MIA. I suppose there's the possibility Timothy may still be alive."

Jack frowned as he leaned against one wall of the elevator. The cold shiver traveling up his spine was a premonition of things to come. He didn't like the sound of that; didn't like the possibility of Timothy coming back to claim Rose.

At the office, Rose became engrossed in the day's work, though she was well aware of Jack's presence when he'd buzz her phone or come out of his office and sit on the edge of her desk with work questions. By the end of the day, she admitted Jack Campbell was too attractive for her peace of mind.

Finding another job would be the best solution. She feared she'd soon accept his marriage proposal if she didn't leave soon. She glanced down at her wedding ring and sighed. Perhaps it was time to remove it, after all, years had passed, and Timothy hadn't returned. Perhaps it was time to allow love into her life again.

At five o'clock Jack strode out of his office, just as she covered her typewriter. He went to the closet, pulled out her coat and said, "I'll wait for you at your house while you change clothes."

She slipped her arms into the sleeves of her coat, feeling confused. "Change clothes? Why?"

"We're having dinner tonight with Aunt Pearl."

"Since I don't have an Aunt Pearl, I'm assuming she's your aunt."

He nodded. "We're picking her up at six." He glanced at his watch and added, "Which only gives you half an hour to change."

"Wouldn't you rather take your aunt to dinner without me?"

"She wants to meet you."

"You told her about me? What did you say?"

"That I've the best secretary in the world." He escorted her from the office and down the hallway.

A pleasurable feeling came over her. "You did?"

"Oh, yes," he said.

Rose lengthened her stride to keep up with him while trying to keep her attention focused on their conversation.

"I also informed her that I'm courting you. Needless to say, this makes her very happy as my family is anxious for me to marry and have children."

Rose's euphoria dissipated and the noose tightened once more just as they reached Jack's car. "But we aren't courting! We're business associates, and that's all."

He soothed her. "I agree, we do work together well, but humor my aunt, won't you? She's seventy-four years old and won't be around forever."

What could she say to that? Humor the woman, indeed! Oh, she'd make Jack pay for this sometime in the very near future.

"If I can find a sitter, I'll come," Rose said in a last-ditch effort to gain control of this spiraling situation.

At her house, Jack allowed Sarah to entertain him with card tricks while Rose changed clothes. She'd wear black this night, to match her mood. She heard the doorbell and knew it was the sitter for Sarah. Rose hurried out of her room, met up with Katie Lynn Donohue, not Sarah's favorite sitter but the teen was responsible and available this evening on short notice.

With a pearl necklace and matching clip earrings in her hand, Rose sank to her knees beside Sarah. She hugged her and said, "Bedtime is eight o'clock, no later, and no arguing with Katie Lynn."

Sarah sighed. "Okay." She noticed the jewelry in her mother's hand and said, "Turn around, Mommy. I'll hook your necklace."

Rose had just started to hand over the pearls when Jack held out his hand. "I'll do the honors, Sarah, if you don't mind."

Sarah gave Jack a radiant smile then turned a mischievous one on her mother but didn't say a word—she didn't have to. Her matchmaker expression said it all.

Rose started to rise when Jack sat down on the sofa and trapped her with his knees. "Stay put. You're the perfect height right where you are."

First chills then heat traveled up Rose's spine when his fingers touched the skin on her neck. As he sat on the sofa, his big body surrounded hers as he hooked the necklace. Then he traced the pearls with one hand until he reached the very center of the strand that suspended near her slight cleavage, exposed by her round-necked dress.

Her voice shook when she said, "Done?"

"Yes," his low voice rumbled but he didn't remove his hand.

Rose came to her feet and Jack had to quickly sit back or be hit on the chin. Rose crossed the room, opened the closet door and retrieved her coat.

Before she could remove it from the hanger he was there, taking the coat and tucking her inside it. Lord, but the man seemed to be everywhere! And his hands were adept at every little chore.

They said their 'good-byes' and he rushed her to his car. Once inside he turned to her, a wicked gleam in his eyes as he took in her dress.

"You are a beautiful woman dressed in black, Miss Rose," he drawled. "You were the first time on our date and now it took all of my willpower to keep my hands to myself inside."

She gasped, "Jack Campbell! I can't possibly meet your aunt tonight dressed in something that's—"

"Scintillating?" he asked and laughed at her appalled expression. "Aunt Pearl will think you're as beautiful as I do and won't notice the fact that you exude passion in that dress, but I sure as heck noticed."

Rose silently cursed herself all the way to Aunt Pearl's house. Where she'd thought basic black would do nothing for her, it seemed Jack thought otherwise.

At the restaurant, Rose thoroughly enjoyed Jack's Aunt Pearl. The conversation held her attention and kept her mind off the fact Jack was staring at her all evening. He didn't say much but she felt his eyes on her often.

By the end of the evening Rose decided Aunt Pearl was one of the most delightful people she'd ever met. And when the woman invited her to her home for Christmas Eve dinner with the rest of the family, Rose was forced to decline the invitation. Finally, looking into the kindly woman's eyes, she said, "I'm sorry. I'll be out of town visiting family over the holidays."

When Rose took in Jack's slack-jawed expression, she realized she hadn't mentioned she had two older sisters living in New York City, both editors, one with a high-fashion magazine, and the other a book editor with a renowned publishing firm. Elaine and Miriam were both married and had three children each, but that hadn't stopped them from achieving remarkable careers. Christmas was the only time Rose and Sarah saw the family.

Jack settled Aunt Pearl into the front seat of his car then opened the back door for Rose, murmuring, "You never told me you had any family."

She smiled at him. "You never asked."

Later, after they'd dropped Aunt Pearl off at her home, Rose moved up front beside Jack. Once they reached Rose's house, Jack parked then turned to face her. Rose saw the intent look in his eyes when he said, "You are coming to the bank's Christmas ball with me, right? It's two weeks from today."

"I said I would. Lord, I can't believe the holidays are nearly upon us again." Five weeks away and she hadn't done a lick of shopping.

He nodded. "Excellent," and engulfed her small hand in his. "How long will you be gone during the holidays?"

"Just a week. Our flight arrives home the morning of December thirtieth."

Jack's smile widened. "Excellent. You'll be here in time to spend New Year's Eve with me. My parents always throw a party. Come, won't you?"

"I'd like that," Rose said without hesitation.

"Wear a costume."

She frowned. "On New Year's?"

"Absolutely. We even pick a theme."

"What's this year's theme?"

"Famous warriors and their counterparts."

Rose grinned. "Counterpart? A queen, perhaps?"

"Queen, maiden, whatever you deem suitable."

She arched one eyebrow. "Have you chosen your costume yet?"

"Yes, but I'm not telling. The best costumes are self-explanatory."

His eyes delved deep into hers. Rose found herself nearly

hugging the passenger door in order to prevent throwing herself into his arms. He leaned toward her and his gaze never left hers as he said softly, "Guess it's time to call it a night. A kiss good night is all I ask, sweetheart."

"You may," she said, with no hesitation. Then she tilted her head back and accepted his kiss. Heat soared through her body as his lips sealed hers.

Rose wasn't certain how long the kiss lasted—not long enough to her way of thinking. Soon Jack was beside her, easing her from her seat, walking her to her door. There he stole another kiss, a fleeting one this time. Then, with a jaunty smile and quick salute he turned on his heel.

She watched his long-limbed stride as he raced to his car. Her back hit the door when she slumped back, eyeing his automobile until it roared away and out of sight. She nearly fell inside her house when the door suddenly opened.

Sarah stood there, a wide-eyed look on her face. "Mom? What are you doing standing outside?" She leaned out further, looked around, then said, "Where's Mr. Campbell?"

"He left," Rose said with a frown. "Why aren't you in bed, young lady?"

"Mother, it's only nine o'clock."

"And way past your bedtime. You've school tomorrow."

Sarah grinned. "Nope. It's Saturday, remember?"

Rose sighed, chastising herself for forgetting the day of the week. If she hadn't been so flustered by the blasted man's kiss, she would have remembered, and would have asked him in for a cup of coffee at the very least, but more than likely would have offered him a glass of wine or a shot of bourbon.

Chagrinned, she made her way to her modest liquor cabinet and poured a thimble-sized glass of sherry. She'd need it if she expected to get any sleep this night.

❄

Jack hated Sunday dinner with his parents, but always attended. His mother would have been disappointed if he hadn't. Why, he couldn't understand since he and his father inevitably tangled with each other.

"Jim Ketchum's retiring at the beginning of the year," Jack's father said.

Jack sighed when he caught the hopeful gleam in his father's eye. Carefully, he set down his fork and leaned back in his chair. "I'm not interested, you know that."

"Why the hell not?" John Campbell shouted, "I'm offering you the Vice-President position, for God's sake, even though you don't know a thing about the business."

"Dear?" Jack's mother said, patting her husband's hand. "This isn't news to you. Jack's told you before he has no desire to join the company."

John yanked his hand from beneath his wife's, balled it into a fist and pounded the table.

She gasped and shrank away. Jack narrowed his eyes on his father, anger building but he managed to keep it simmering inside him instead of exploding, knowing well it would do no good; knowing well maintaining his own temper leveled his father's.

"This is my last offer inviting you to come in with me. Are you in or not?" John growled.

Without hesitation, Jack said softly, "I'll prove to you soon, once and for all, I can make it on my own. Count-me-out." Jack rose, then turned to his mother. "Sorry, Mom. I'll talk to you soon." His leg was more sore than usual, and he limped to the door.

From the dining room he heard his father shout, "You come back here, Jeanne. Leave him go, now, you've coddled that boy enough!" His father's scoffing voice added, "We'll see if he proves himself or not, won't we?"

On the sidewalk leading to his car Jack paused when he

heard his mother cry out his name. He whirled around and found her standing in the doorway, tears flooding her eyes.

"Don't be angry," she begged. "You know what he's like."

Jack sighed, put on a happy front. "No need to worry, Mother. I understand him better than you think. Lunch on Friday okay with you?"

Her lips quivered even as they turned up into a smile. "Yes, I'd love that."

He nodded. "I'll meet you at Donovan's Grill at eleven-thirty. And I'll have a guest with me."

Her smile widened. "Your lady—what did you say was her name?"

"Rose."

"Yes, Rose! I'll enjoy meeting her."

On his way home Jack passed Rose's house, having decided he'd propose marriage again. With the ever-growing pressure from his father, the extra measure of stability in his life would prove he was strong and knew his own mind—knew what he wanted in life—and he didn't want the same things as his father.

He shouldn't stop unannounced and passed right by Rose's house. At the corner, though, he turned, drove around the block, then pulled up in front of her small house. As he exited his car he heard Sarah's laughter from near the back of the house.

He strode in that direction, paused before an old rickety wood gate and grinned when he found Rose playing catch with Sarah. He was astonished to see her legs concealed beneath a pair of blue dungarees and a huge sweatshirt covered her curves. The huge glove on her hand let him know it had been built for a man, and not for this slight woman.

"Mr. Campbell!" Sarah shouted, tore off her glove and ran to him.

He reached down, tapped her nose and grinned. "Want me to give you some batting tips?"

"Sure thing!" she exclaimed and opened the gate. "Mom! Look who's here."

"I can see, Sarah."

Jack heard the cool tone in Rose's voice and schooled his grin. *Now what was wrong?*

He hesitated. "Is that okay?"

Rose shrugged and passed him the glove as she started to stride by him. He reached out, held her in place in front of him. "Stay put," he muttered, "I might need some pointers here."

She laughed at the pained expression on his face. "You offered, but don't have to do this, you know."

"I know. But I want to."

Uncertainty crossed her face. "It doesn't appear that way to me. Been a long time since you tossed a ball around?"

"It has, but that's not the problem. It's just that, well, sometimes I'm not sure how to speak to your daughter. I haven't spent much time with kids, in general."

Rose raised her brows. "Really? I've a suggestion then."

"I'm all ears."

"Just turn on the charm as you do each time you see me. It'll work on Sarah, I can guarantee it," she said dryly.

Jack chuckled. "So, you're saying my charm is difficult to resist."

"Now that's an understatement if I ever heard one." With a sigh she said, "I was just heading in to make supper, anyway."

That gave him pause. And while he'd love to have her invite him in, even though he'd stuffed himself at his parents' home, he guessed she wouldn't make the offer. But he'd be damned if he tried to coerce an invitation out of her. He wanted this woman to come to him of her own free will.

"Okay. I'll play with Sarah until you're ready to call her in to eat."

She gave him a suspicious look. "You're being mighty amiable today."

He shrugged. "No more than usual."

"What have you up your sleeve now?" she groaned.

"Later, darling," he murmured.

Rose groaned, "You can't leave me suspended like this, Jack!"

"Curious, are you?" At her nod he added, "I've another plan in mind for us. How about a long engagement?"

Sarah's eyes widened and she whispered, "Engagement? You mean like in before getting married engagement?"

"Yes." He took Rose's hand. As she stood at his side he raised it to his lips and kissed it.

Another *be still my heart* entered Rose's mind even as she tried to find the words to give him a negative reply.

"Don't say 'no' until you've heard me out."

After a long while she gave a brief nod, stayed at his side.

"I've been thinking about this a lot, lately, so don't think this was an impetuous idea."

"Give me one good reason for me to accept," Rose said.

"I can make your life easier."

Now how was any sane woman supposed to answer that? Easier? What temptation! Life had never been easy for Rose. Working full time, shuffling her daughter off to babysitters and then early school, and paying bills and balancing a household budget. But then she reasoned her life wasn't much different than other women during wartimes.

Another voice roared through her consciousness then. *But what about love?* "Let me think about it."

CHAPTER 8

Thanksgiving Day, 1946

Jack's body went taut as he clenched his fists at his sides and stormed from his parents' home. He was ready to pop the first person he met, right smack in the kisser. Damn his father!

As he strode to his car he glanced back at the imposing Colonial home where he'd grown up, expecting to see his mother's sad face in the doorway but saw no sign of her. As he settled behind the wheel, he was disappointed she hadn't watched him leave. Jack's father likely was holding her back, not with physical restraints, but with his form of emotional abuse of which Jack was inordinately familiar since he'd been the recipient of the same treatment growing up.

The old man had a way of making his mother feel guilty about his poor relationship with his only child. Jack wanted to confront the man once and for all, but his mother hadn't wanted him to, knowing it would only worsen things. For now Jack had kept the peace by leaving the house whenever he and his father had disagreements.

Jack couldn't recall the last time he'd enjoyed a visit and a meal with both of his parents. He and his mother always had a good time together, but his dour father was always serious, quick to anger and distracted, physically present but emotionally absent. Not for the first time did Jack wonder about his paternal grandparents who'd died years before he'd been born. What sort of people had they been to have raised a man of high principals and work ethic but incapable of loving.

He started the engine. Just when he pressed down and popped the clutch pain shot through his injured thigh. As he tried to relax the limb with the Charlie horse, he decided he'd have to pay another visit to the doctor soon to find out if the shrapnel had moved. The pain was coming more often and growing worse, but usually after he'd experienced some measure of stress and anger. As he drove home he tried to relax and gather peace around him.

"Are you ready to leave, Sarah?" Rose called up the stairs.

"Almost, Mommy! I'm trying to find my apron with the turkey on the front!"

"I've got your apron, honey, right here with mine. We've got to hurry if we want to make the eleven-thirty streetcar downtown."

Sarah clattered down the wood steps and Rose smiled at her. How grown up she appeared in her plaid red wool jumper and matching tam on her head.

Rose said, "Remember last year when I said I'd keep them stored in the closet together so we'd have them for next year?"

"I forgot."

They left the house and walked down the snowy sidewalk until Sarah couldn't hold in her happiness and scampered away. "Don't get too far ahead of me, honey!" she called. Sarah didn't reply but skipped through the snow. She'd just reached the corner when an automobile turned too sharp, slid and crashed into the curb, directly in front of Sarah, causing her to shriek and jump back. Thankfully, the car had come to a stop and Sarah was safe on the sidewalk.

"Sarah!" Rose finally managed to shout as she met up with her on the corner. There she clasped Sarah against her chest.

Rose glared at the automobile which had stopped headfirst in a bank of snow when she realized it looked familiar. Sure, there were hundreds of Studebakers like Jack Campbell's but his was the only one she'd ever noticed on her block. She took a few steps toward the automobile and peered inside, gasping when she saw that it was indeed Jack, leaning heavily over the steering wheel.

"Run home, Sarah! Here's the key. Call the police for help!"

Sarah looked with wide eyes between the automobile and her mother, then hurried away.

Rose moved around to the driver's side and opened the door. Her hand shook when she reached inside and gently stroked Jack's forehead resting against the steering wheel. "Jack?"

Slowly, his head came up and Rose nearly sobbed at the horrified, white faced expression on his face. "Is—is Sarah okay?"

Rose nodded. "She's fine. What happened? Did you hit an icy patch?"

Jack shook his head. "No. Once in a while I get a really bad cramp in my injured leg and the pain is excruciating. It's never happened before while driving. I'll have to pay attention for early signs of it in the future." He sank against the back of the seat and threw one forearm over his eyes, breathing heavily.

"Come back to the house with me. You need to rest a bit."

Slowly, he lowered his arm, met her eyes. "You are something else, sweetheart, do you know that?"

She frowned. "What do you mean?"

"My God, I almost killed your daughter and you're worried about me." He gave a mirthless laugh. "Shoot me, why don't you? Put me out of my misery."

Rose's heart clenched at the torment in his voice. She knew little of his injuries and wasn't sure what to say, how to approach him about it, when she decided being straightforward was the only thing she could do.

"Stop talking nonsense, now, and come back to the house with me."

"Tell me you forgive me for scaring you and Sarah."

She sighed. "If it makes you feel better, fine, we forgive you. Now then, please, come along."

"Let me drive to your house. I can't leave my car here."

For a moment, Rose bit her lip, then said, "Are you sure you can drive?"

"Positive."

"I'll meet you there."

She turned and ran toward her house, clutching her camel wool coat against her body, protecting her from the wind and light snow that was falling. Her short, black boots protected her feet and she reached the house at the same moment Jack pulled up on the opposite side of the street. After he stumbled from his car she met him, wound an arm around his waist, and he flung his arm around her shoulders. She guided him across the street and up the sidewalk to her house. Rose noticed his limp was even more pronounced than usual and she wondered about his injuries.

Once she'd settled him in a deep, comfortable chair she lit the fire she'd made earlier in the day to warm him. From her kneeling position before the hearth she turned and found him staring at her. His gaze was hot, penetrating the cold in her body. She rose swiftly and said, "I'll get you a hot toddy."

"Bourbon. Have you any?"

She nodded thought of a bottle Timothy had bought but had never been opened.

"It works best at alleviating the pain," he explained.

"Of course," she muttered, then made her way to the opposite corner where her liquor cabinet stood. She poured him half a tumbler full of the whiskey, sped across the room and handed him the glass. She watched him toss down the drink, ignored the potency of it, then sank back against the chair. His breathing was deep, heavy, and she worried anew about his condition.

Relief flooded through her when an ambulance arrived. As the experienced emergency workers assessed Jack's condition she found herself biting her lip to prevent outright laughter from escaping at the anger and impatience in Jack. Obviously, he was not happy Sarah had called for help. When the men were convinced he was fine they left.

Jack glared at Sarah. "You little stinker. Were you the one who called in the forces?"

Her eyes widened on him as a worried expression crossed her small, pale face. "Mommy told me to," she whispered.

Rose caught his gentle smile on her daughter and found herself smiling in return. Then he looked at Rose and said, "Mommy was right. Thank you."

Sarah looked at her mother. "So, are we going to stay with Mr. Campbell instead of serving at the mission?"

Jack scowled. "You were going to serve Thanksgiving dinner to the poor today?"

Rose nodded. "We do every year."

"You don't eat with family, then?"

"My family lives out of state so there wouldn't be enough time. I've never been able to take extra time off from work for both Thanksgiving and Christmas so, we usually do this, instead. It's a worthwhile experience. We've met some very interesting people over the years at our Thanksgiving dinner, haven't we Sarah?"

Sarah grinned and nodded.

"Sarah's learned to appreciate that there are people in the world who do need help and is far less self-centered than other children because of it."

Gruffly, Jack said, waving his hand in the air, "Don't let me stop you." He started to rise.

"We're you on the way to your family's home?"

"No," Jack said, "I'd already been there. Mother and I attend church services together on Sundays and holidays. We'd just returned home when, well, all hell broke loose, guess you'd say."

She gasped. "Is everything all right?"

"Sure." Jack shrugged then and added, "It was typical. Dad picked a fight with me so I left before we'd finished eating. I suppose I should go back, for Mother's sake."

"Of course, perhaps that would be best. But, I know the mission can always use more help on a day like today. You're welcome to join us."

Jack grinned. "I can't think of a better thing to do. I'll come along if you don't mind."

"Yeah, Mr. Campbell!" Sarah shouted. She reached out, took his hand and tried hauling him from the chair. He helped her, of course, under the guise of allowing her to think she'd performed the Herculean task herself.

At the mission, after they'd stood on their feet for a solid two hours and served plates heaping with turkey, mashed potatoes and gravy and sweet potatoes and green beans, they finally sank into seats themselves to eat. All three of them felt good about themselves and the good deed they'd accomplished, though not a word about it was mentioned.

Soon guilt seeped into Jack's consciousness as he thought about how lucky he'd been in life having been born into wealth; surviving the war; having family, even his father, especially as he watched today as weary-eyed strangers ate their holiday dinner with other strangers.

He made a solemn vow to try and be more appreciative of his father. And, it appeared luck was on his side since he'd been able to spend the day with Rose and her daughter. Then he recalled his request for a long engagement, having proposed to Rose a few weeks back. She'd yet to give him an answer other than, 'I'll think about it'. If she accepted, he'd already decided that a four-month long engagement would have to suffice since he had big plans for spring.

He'd press her about it again when he dropped her off at her house today. Soon he'd have to secure his inheritance in order to begin his home-building business. He'd already put a down payment on a parcel of land, with the intention of building houses on it in the spring but couldn't proceed unless he had his grandmother's money in the bank.

But, the money was only one reason to marry sweet Rose. He knew he loved her and couldn't live without her in his life. He just had to convince the marriage-shy woman of the fact.

When they arrived at her house, Sarah ran next door to play with a friend while Rose and Jack sat in front of the fireplace with warmed mulled toddies in hand.

After Jack had exhausted his idea of small talk with her, and Rose had relaxed now that the hectic day was nearing its end, he decided being forthright now would benefit him.

She sat beside him on the small sofa. They'd kicked off their shoes and had crossed their ankles on the coffee table positioned in front of them, relaxed, comfortable with each other.

"Marry me, Rose."

She turned a wide-eyed look on him. "Oh! I thought you'd forgotten about it," she said nervously.

He heard the trembling in her voice, knew she wasn't comfortable talking about it. He took the hand that was now busily tucking strands of hair behind her ears.

"I've dreams of what I'd enjoy doing with you as my wife. I won't share those dreams with you until after I've a ring on your finger, and we've said our 'I Do's'."

Rose sighed and leaned into him, gently laid her head on his shoulder. "You are very good at tempting me, you know."

He chuckled. "Give me one good reason why we shouldn't marry."

Relief tore through him when, after a while, she didn't give him a negative reply but said, instead, "It's been nearly six years since Timothy left."

"Rose, I don't want to hurt you but there's little chance he's coming back."

"I know," she said softly. After a long while she added, "I know you'll be a fine husband, Jack Campbell."

He gently pulled her away from him. As he faced her on the sofa, he took her shoulders in his hands. "Are you saying yes?"

She gave him a trembling smile and nodded.

"You sure about this?"

"Sure as I'll ever be, I guess."

"I am looking forward to you being home, tending our house, waiting for my arrive home every night with supper on the table and a fine cognac in hand for me. I Imagine you dressed in one of those pretty colorful sweaters and skirts I've seen you wear, with Sarah at the table, the three of us enjoying a relaxing meal together." Jack knew he'd convinced her to marry him when tears flooded her eyes.

"You paint a very pretty picture, you know. And what if Timothy is still alive?"

"If, in the future, this proves to be true, but I highly doubt it, then we'll deal with the problem."

"Yes, I'll be your wife," she said as one tear slipped down her cheek.

Jack grinned ear to ear. "Thank you, sweetheart. You'll

never regret a day of being married to me. I promise." He reached inside his pocket and withdrew a black velvet box.

Rose gasped at the exquisite white gold diamond ring set with a large square diamond in the center and two smaller square-shaped diamonds on either side.

She stared at it, eyes wide, until Jack laughed, pulled the ring from the box and gently eased it on her finger, after first removing her wedding band from Timothy.

Rose held Timothy's ring and bit her lip, knowing she was taking a huge step in her life, but didn't regret it. It felt right getting engaged to Jack. And they sealed their bargain in the way men and women have done through the ages—with a fervent kiss.

CHAPTER 9

December 1946

C hristmas shopping in downtown St. Paul was both a
chore and a treat for Rose. She thoroughly enjoyed
Sarah's visit with Santa at Macy's each year but hated the
crowded shops and the waiting in line to pay for merchandise.
Rose had little money to purchase things so she spent much
time trying to find the perfect gifts for her sisters and their
families, within her meager budget.

Sarah was easier to shop for since she always seemed to
have an on-going list of toys she'd dearly love and, thankfully,
ones Rose could afford.

Rose sighed as she trudged through the new fallen snow
covering the sidewalk as she made her way to the next
department store. Each holiday season, she'd shop over
several days during the month of December, having budgeted
a bit of money from each paycheck since she never had
enough money to shop in one outing, much as that was her
preference.

Thankfully, because it was only a week until Christmas,
the crowds had lessened somewhat, the earlier shoppers

having finished their shopping. She'd left Sarah home with her next-door neighbor because Rose planned on purchasing toys for her daughter.

Rose found herself relaxing a bit, now that her shopping was near completion. She took in the twinkling, colorful lights strung over light poles and rimming store windows. She paused in front of a multi-paned glass and grinned at the display of toys there. She had her eye on a doll carriage, but knew it was not within her price range since she'd already checked on it earlier in the month on one of her other shopping trips. Then her eyes settled on the two-story dollhouse and she sighed, knowing this was at the top of Sarah's list, but also unaffordable.

She turned to enter the store to decide on a few other, less expensive toys when someone bumped into her. She would have tumbled to the ground except a hard hand grasped her, then she heard a man's low voice apologize, "Sorry, miss."

She turned, looked up and met the scowling visage of a handsome, elderly man who looked remarkably like an older version of Jack Campbell.

He released her arm and said, "Are you all right? Didn't mean to bump into you like that, but I wasn't anticipating you turning so abruptly away from that window."

"Oh! I'm sorry, too, sir."

His expression softened and then he glanced through the windowpane. "Haven't been around a toyshop in years," he muttered.

Rose noticed his silvery temples, but the rest of his hair appeared as dark as Jack's, and his features resembled Jack's as well. My gosh, this man had to be Jack's father since the likeness was uncanny.

"You going inside?" he said. When she didn't reply, he narrowed his eyes. "Cat got your tongue, miss?" And then, "Are you okay?"

She couldn't help but laugh outright at his remark. His straightforward manners reminded her of Jack.

"I'm fine. Yes, I'm going inside to shop for my daughter."

"How old is she?"

"Nearly five but going on fourteen."

The man grinned, but didn't look comfortable, as though grinning was something he didn't often do.

"What would she like?"

Rose laughed. "Oh, I know what she'd like." She pointed at the carriage and then at the dollhouse. "She's wanted the dollhouse since she saw it in this store last Christmas, but it's seventy dollars, which means it's definitely not in my budget."

"That's too bad."

"Yes, it is, but she understands."

The man reached inside his pocket and pulled out a thick wad of money. He pressed it into her nerveless fingers and said, "Here. Make this the best Christmas she's ever had."

"But I can't take your money, sir!" Rose protested.

"You'll make me a very happy man if you do. I've no grandchildren and may never have any. Make an old man happy, won't you? I'll give you my name and address. I'd like you to take a photograph of your daughter with the dollhouse on Christmas morning. That's all I ask."

Rose sniffed. "That's all?" At his nod she added, "Thank you. I'll think of you always whenever Sarah plays with it. And you'll have your picture shortly after Christmas, but I'll need your name and address."

"Have you a piece of paper in your bag?"

Rose produced a small tablet and handed it to him along with a fountain pen.

He held the pen, but his eyes were riveted on her left hand. "Is something wrong?" she asked.

"Your engagement ring. At least, I think it's one. Am I correct?"

Heat seeped into Rose's cheeks as she nodded.

"It's familiar."

She laughed. "Oh, I'm certain you'd likely find this ring in just about any jeweler's store, don't you think?"

He shrugged. "Perhaps." Quickly, he dashed off his personal information and returned the items to her. With a half-smile and a jaunty tip of his fedora he turned and strode away. Only after she'd lost sight of him did she look down at the paper and gasped when she saw a name scrawled boldly there. John Campbell.

Five days before Christmas

Because Rose and Sarah would be gone over Christmas to visit her sisters in New York City, Rose invited Jack over to help them decorate a small tree and eat dinner.

He arrived early afternoon and hauled the few boxes of ornaments Rose had in the basement into the living room.

Within a short time since the tree was small and the ornaments were few, they had the tree decorated. Jack plugged in the lights and he laughed at Sarah's squeals of delight. She stood in front of the tree wide-eyed and clapping her hands.

They ate a simple dinner of roast chicken, mashed potatoes and gravy and asparagus.

"This is the best meal I've had in a long time," Jack said enthusiastically as he set down his fork and rubbed his stomach.

Rose smiled, thinking how his stomach looked as flat as before he began eating. He was not only naturally slim, but she also knew he worked out, enhancing his physique. Of course, his over six feet height helped hide the pounds, unlike her little over five feet in height; she put on a pound and it immediately appeared, especially in her butt and hips. She sighed, thinking of the unfairness of it, but you can't fight genetics.

"Oh, I'm pretty sure you've had plenty of great meals at your folks' house," she said. "Don't they have a professional cook on staff?"

"Sure, and Suzette's French cooking is great but there's nothing better in my mind than American home cooking like yours."

After they cleaned up the kitchen and Rose washed the dishes and Jack dried them, they moseyed into the living room and put on *It's a Wonderful Life*, which all of them had seen before but enjoyed as if it were the first time they watched it. Just before the movie ended, Sarah fell asleep.

Rose was glad she had her daughter don her pjs's before the movie began. When she bent over to pick up Sarah for bed Jack moved Rose aside.

"Let me. She's too heavy for you."

"Okay, thanks," she whispered.

Jack easily carried Sarah to her bed. Afterward, he sank down on the sofa with Rose, pulling her onto his lap and kissing her fervently.

Rose's heart seemed to race with each kiss, and she knew, if she didn't slow things down, they'd end this race in a way they might both regret—in a way she wasn't sure she was ready for—though Jack certainly appeared to be.

Pulling her head back and pushing his hands down from around her she scrambled from his lap and sat beside him.

"Not with Sarah in the house," she murmured.

Jack frowned, then sighed. "I want to take you to bed. I want to make love to you. We are engaged, after all."

"Yes, but with Sarah in the room beside mine, I wouldn't feel, well, comfortable."

"You've told me she's a sound sleeper and she knows we're getting married. I'm sure she wouldn't find it odd to see us in bed together."

"You're probably right," Rose began, "but—"

Jack came to his feet and picked her up in his arms as easily as he had Sarah. Then he strode down the hall to her room.

"Wait, Jack, let's talk about this."

"No talking. We've been talking since we met. Stop thinking, too. Seems to slow down our moving forward."

"Jack!"

He dumped her on her bed and followed her down. He made amazingly short work of pulling off her clothes, then his own before settling them both beneath the covers.

Rose blew her bangs back off her forehead. "Never have I seen a person move as fast as you."

"You haven't seen nothing yet," he warned.

Taking her in his arms, he kissed her until her lips felt bruised. He stroked her body until she realized why cats loved that kind of attention. And when he angled himself up and over her, pressing her down in the bed, she wound her arms around him.

He paused, looked down at her and stroked one cheek. "You okay, sweetheart?"

"Yes, it's just been a while."

"Tell me if you need me to slow down."

She gazed up at his stark features, saw his eyes dark with desire. "And what if I asked you to stop?" she said softly.

She saw his Adam's apple bob, then he replied, "I'd hate to, but I could—I would for you—if you truly wanted me to. Do you want me to stop?"

Rose shook her head as a wide smile formed on her lips. "Not a chance, soldier."

On December 23, Sarah and Rose flew out of Minneapolis–St. Paul Metropolitan Airport and arrived in New York City four hours later. Rose held Sarah's hand and steered her around the crowd of passengers until they entered an open area on the concourse. She spotted her sisters, Elaine and Miriam, waiting near a window and waved her hand high to gain their attention.

"Look!" Sarah shouted, "Aunt Miriam and Aunt Elaine!" She hurried away to meet them.

Miriam swept the fair-haired Sarah into her arms and grinned. "Just look how much you've grown in a year."

Soon Rose and Sarah were surrounded by family. Rose was delighted by the welcoming group; just her sisters' husbands were missing and each of their two youngest children, likely because they were back at Miriam's house. Her sisters had each given birth to another baby in the past three months. To look at her pretty, slim sisters, one would never guess they'd been with child just a few short months ago. Rose could hardly wait to tell them about her engagement.

"You all look wonderful," Rose said wistfully. "And it's so good to see you again!"

"Likewise," Miriam replied. "Sure glad you're a good letter writer since your visits are so far and between."

Rose's sisters each grabbed one of her arms and started walking quickly toward a tiny café with red leather-topped stools lined up before a counter. The children, Sarah's oldest cousins, Lucinda and Mary, twelve and thirteen who'd been tailing them, took seats at the counter while Rose and her sisters sat at a table. Once they placed their orders, hot chocolate for the adults and phosphates for the children, they chatted happily, laughter mixed with shouts of delight in their conversation. Suddenly, Miriam screamed, "Elaine, look at Rose's hand."

"You're engaged?" Elaine whispered her eyes riveted on Rose's diamond ring.

Rose nodded and grinned at the same time. "Recently."

"To whom and when's the date?" Elaine asked.

"His name is Jack Campbell and we haven't set a date yet. I've been working at the bank in his stead while he's been away at war. He's returned and has assumed his job."

Miriam said, "But what will you do for work?"

"Jack hired me as his secretary." She held up her hand to ward off protests. "I know, it's not accounting work but I'm lucky to have the secretary job since I haven't found another job in accounting."

"Does it really matter since you're marrying him?" Elaine said. "After all, you'll likely stay home and keep house for him, won't you?"

Rose shrugged. "That's what Jack would like me to do. It'll be a novelty, for certain since I've never had the pleasure of being a housewife."

"What sort of wedding will you have?" Miriam asked.

"We'll keep it small and simple, just family I suspect since this is my second marriage, although it's Jack's first."

Miriam's smile slipped. "Have you received word about Timothy?"

Rose shook her head and bit her lip, waiting for the explosion she knew would surely follow.

"But what if he's alive?" Miriam exclaimed.

"As Jack would say, we'll address the problem if and when it happens."

The sisters sighed and, from the faraway look in their eyes, Rose knew they were thinking about their own marriage vows they'd taken years ago.

Finally, Elaine said, "I wish Momma and Poppa were still alive and could see how happy you are, Rose."

Rose swallowed the growing lump in her throat, thinking how unfair it was that her parents had been taken from them in an awful automobile accident ten years ago. Rose was the youngest of the three sisters and had just graduated from high school a few weeks before the ill-fated accident. Her sisters had already married by then.

"I do too," Rose said softly, blinking back her tears. Then she smiled through them and added, "Hey, no one's going to rain on my parade! I'm happy as a lark, and as soon as we set the date I'll let you know. You're going to love him I just know it."

Two hours later they arrived at Miriam's home in Brooklyn, in time to share a wonderful Christmas Eve dinner of roast turkey and gravy, mashed potatoes, sweet potatoes, corn and rolls, and mince and apple pies. After the meal Rose sank back in her chair at the dining room table and rubbed her stomach.

Groaning, she said, "I just can't eat a bite more."

"Me neither," said Sarah. "When are we going to open presents?"

Elaine leaned across the table and smiled at Sarah. "We don't open presents until Christmas Day, Sarah. You know that."

"I know," Sarah grumbled, "but Mommy lets me open one present on Christmas Eve."

"Sorry, kiddo," Elaine said, "We wait until Christmas Day."

"Who's up for some carol-singing?" Harry, Elaine's husband asked as he entered the living room, baby Robert in his arms, and their toddler, Charlie alongside him.

"I am!" Sarah shouted,

"Me too," others chorused.

Harry passed the baby to Elaine then strode across the living room toward the piano. Once he'd pulled out the bench and sank onto the cushioned seat, he proceeded to play a rousing rendition of 'Jingle Bells' and everyone sang along.

Tears gathered in Rose's eyes when, after they'd nearly sang their voices raw, Harry played the soft, melancholy

'Silent Night'. Though she was surrounded by her loving family Rose felt lost and at loose ends this evening.

Much later, after the children had gone to bed, Rose imbibed in a glass of champagne with her sisters and their husbands. But once she retired to the guestroom and readied herself for bed, sadness lingered inside her still.

The lonely feeling didn't leave her until she realized why she'd been feeling this way; she missed Jack. Somehow, Christmas without her fiancé just wasn't festive as it should be. She missed him dreadfully and, after checking her watch, she decided it wasn't too late to call him and wish him a Merry Christmas.

Rose stole downstairs and dialed his number on the telephone sitting on the end of the kitchen counter. She sighed when Jack didn't answer. He must still be with his family, she thought. She'd try him again in the morning.

The children woke much earlier than their parents' would have wanted them to, but they fully understood their excitement. As Rose, her sisters and their husbands stumbled downstairs at eight o'clock Christmas Day, Rose took a detour into the kitchen where she once again placed a call to Jack. This time he answered, and boy, did he sound grumpy!

"Uh, hi Jack. Did I wake you?"

She didn't understand his reply. He sounded half asleep and his voice was muffled, as though he were sleeping on his stomach with his mouth smashed into his pillow.

"It's Rose. I'm sorry I called so early, but…"

"Rose!" he happily shouted.

She heard a rustling noise followed by a murmured curse. She cringed, then relaxed when he said, "I miss you, sweetheart."

"I miss you, too," she softly replied. She sank down on a

kitchen chair, rested her elbows on the oak tabletop. "I tried calling you around ten last evening."

"Got in after eleven, or so."

"How did things go with your family?"

"Oh, just swimmingly," he said.

"That's—"

"Hell, it was awful."

"Oh, Jack, what happened?"

"The same thing that happens every year! My father behaves like a big cheese, especially in front of all the relatives. He's obnoxious, boisterous, spends lavish moments kissing my aunts and uncles and gifting them with expensive gifts. He ignores my mother, makes a complete a—"

"Uh, you don't have to say any more. I understand."

"Sorry, don't mean to complain, but my disappointment is too keen to ignore. Ah, hell, what did I expect? Like I said, it's the same every year. Wish I were there with you."

"So do I. We're having a wonderful time."

"Give me your flight number and time of arrival so I know when to pick you up day after tomorrow."

She provided the information then said, "My family's excited about meeting you. I don't dare pay another visit without you at my side."

"I feel the same way. Tell Sarah I wished her a merry one, too. We'll celebrate together after you get back."

"Okay. See you later."

"Before we hang up, did you call for another reason besides wishing me a happy holiday?" he said.

"No, er—well, I just wanted to say I miss you, and—"

"Go ahead," he said gently, "tell me the rest. By the way, you have no idea how much I miss you."

"I miss you," she repeated, "Love you and will see you in a couple days."

"Did you say…?"

Darn it! Jack mused and slammed the telephone down.

Rose had hung up when he had important things to talk to her about. He scowled then a slow grin replaced it. He lay back on his bed, crossed his arms behind his head and thought about Rose's words. He'd heard her slip in the 'love you'. She hadn't given him a chance to reciprocate, but he'd remedy the problem the moment he saw her again.

Then he thought about the one time they'd made love. What a beautiful experience. They'd have that experience again, and again...making Rose his wife couldn't come soon enough, though. He frowned, thinking how she was a very traditional woman, and coercing her into bed hadn't been easy, but when he wouldn't leave their 'nest' at her house, she really had no choice. Like in business, he was tenacious going after what he wanted. Rose wasn't business, but better than business; he wanted her. She wouldn't escape him as he'd set his heart on her.

CHAPTER 10

December 30, 1946
Minneapolis–St. Paul Metropolitan Airport

T he airplane rolled to a stop on the airport tarmac. After receiving direction from the stewardess, Rose and Sarah removed their seatbelts, stood and made their way off the plane. Inside the terminal, they'd taken just a few steps when Rose heard a man's voice shout out to them.

"Rose, Sarah!"

Jack was there, waiting for them. Upon reaching them, he swept them both up into a crushing embrace. He released Sarah but kept Rose in his arms. "Love you," he whispered, then brushed her lips sweetly.

She pulled back, gave him a confused look. "Um, did I hear you correctly?"

"You heard me. I love you. When do you want to get married?"

Rose's mind shouted, *now,* but she didn't want to appear too eager so she said, "How about in early summer, after Sarah is done with school?"

She wondered at the frown on Jack's face until he spoke.

"I was thinking by late March or early April, around the time the ground thaws."

What in the world did ground thaw have to do with the timing of their wedding? She didn't ask but noted his sincere expression and said, "Fine, if that's what you want. I was thinking of a very small wedding, intimate, just family."

He grinned and gave her a big, smacking kiss. "That's fine with me. The day can't come soon enough. Have you eaten lunch yet?"

She shook her head.

"Let's stop by Cheryl's Café for a sandwich."

"Oh, wow!" Sarah exclaimed. "Can I have a chocolate milkshake?"

"Sarah!" Rose chided.

Jack ducked down and tapped Sarah's nose. "You may have two if you want."

Sarah grinned, gave her mother a smug look.

Rose rolled her eyes and scowled at Jack. "You spoil her."

"'Course I do. After all, she's going to be my little girl in a few short months."

He coiled an arm around Rose again and whispered in her ear, "And maybe, if I'm lucky, we'll have even more children."

Heat seeped into Rose's cheeks as she gave him a little shove and a nervous laugh. He smiled at her look of embarrassment but threw back his head and laughed outright when she said, "Be careful what you wish for, Jack Campbell."

December 30, 1946
Mobile, Alabama

Timothy Delaney watched his bride to be head down the church aisle, even as guilt niggled at his conscience. Why, he couldn't say, and while he loved Margaret, his bride, something nagged at him that things weren't right, in his past. Of course, not being able to remember much of his past didn't help matters. For all he knew he'd left a wife behind in Minnesota, having learned that was his birthplace but he had no living kin. Yet when he called public records in Minnesota they couldn't find a marriage license.

After spending months in the hospital in Honolulu after being injured at Pearl Harbor, he'd fallen in love with his nurse, Margaret.

Luckily, he'd managed to find his birth certificate and his driver license, dog tags and release papers from the service in his personal possessions, but that's it, no other documents or pictures.

Timothy had made plans to be with Margaret in the future. Upon his release from the hospital they flew to Margaret's home in Mobile, Alabama.

Timothy had always been lucky in life and now, with his new bride, he was satisfied that his luck hadn't changed.

December 31, 1946

"Are you having a good time, sweetheart?" Jack said.

"Oh, yes," Rose replied, smiling at Jack who sat beside her, one arm draped across the back of her chair.

They were attending his family's New Year's Eve party and Rose couldn't recall when she'd had such a good time. Happy she'd managed to save enough money to purchase the slim columned silver satin dress she wore, she gazed at Jack, dressed in a tuxedo and he looked very suave and sophisticated. This New Year's event of his family's was formal, and she felt as though she fit right in.

Her smile widened as she thought of the shock and

surprise on John Campbell's face when Jack, upon their arrival, escorted her into O'Shaughnessy Golf Club's ballroom. The older man didn't let on that he'd met Rose before, but later, when she'd been walking down the hallway toward the powder room, he'd intercepted her and asked how her daughter had enjoyed the dollhouse and griped he still hadn't received a photograph.

She told him the film was at the developers. As soon as it was developed she promised she'd put the photograph in the mail to him. That satisfied him.

He'd walked her back to the ballroom and then proceeded to dance with her. Rose liked Jack's father but knew the two of them didn't get along. Perhaps she'd be able to breach the void between them once she and Jack married.

Toward midnight, Jack rose from his chair and smiled down at her. "Come on, let's dance."

She caught the glittering, intent look in his eyes when he added, "I can't wait to hold you in my arms again. Hell, I don't know if I'll be able to wait another day let alone three more months to marry you, sweetheart."

Rose laughed when he took her hand and pulled her along behind him to the dance floor. As he swept her into his arms and held her close, she sighed and laid her cheek against his chest. Oh, how she loved the natural, manly scent of him, she mused as she relaxed in his arms. He was tall, handsome, kind, gentle—and persuasive. A small voice inside her asked, *hadn't she learned a thing after rushing in and marrying Timothy?*

She chose to ignore the voice inside—she didn't want to listen—didn't want to hear she could be making a mistake; that she should date Jack, be his girlfriend for a while longer and not marry him so soon. But she didn't listen; she wanted to marry him, would marry him now, at this very moment, except that his mother had insisted they have a bit more formal, larger wedding than they'd first talked of having. Jack was, after all, her only son. Rose had reluctantly agreed and had cheered the woman greatly after giving her carte blanche to plan the entire event, set for April 10th.

Rose and Jack danced several slow, easy dances, until the music grew lively, the songs playing at a faster beat. Jack would never be able to dance to faster music, but that was fine with Rose. The slow, sweet dances were all that mattered to either of them.

As Jack escorted Rose back to their table, he leaned over and whispered, "It's almost midnight, so stay with me to ring in the New Year."

Rose paused beside her chair, thankful theirs was only a table for two and not more. She reached up and placed her hand against his cheek. "I wouldn't miss it for the world, but I do need to pay a visit to the powder room. I'll be right back."

"You'd better be," Jack growled, "or I'm afraid I'll make a scene and barge right into that powder room."

She laughed, swept up her skirts and made her way down the hallway leading to the powder room.

Sadly, Rose learned the meaning of 'marrying when the ground thaws' moments later. Just as she reached the powder room door, which stood ajar, she paused and couldn't help but hear the conversation inside.

"Do you think the dear girl knows about Jack's motives in proposing?" said one woman. Rose stood, rigid, her heart pounding in shock.

"I don't know, Velma. That look in Jack's eyes whenever he watches Rose is, well, it's wonderful." She sighed. "I wish a guy would look at me with so much feeling."

"Oh, come on, Agnes. You know what a flirt Jack's always been. He's had more than his share of the ladies hanging on his every word, from the time he was in seventh grade. He's a charmer, no doubt about it."

Agnes sighed. "You're right, of course. Since I'm his cousin I've seen him turn on the charm on several occasions, but I still think there's something different about his feelings for Rose."

Rose had heard enough and felt ready to burst. She stepped inside and both women looked up, met her eyes with guilty expressions on their faces.

"So, tell me about Jack's motives for marrying me, ladies. I've a right to know," she said, hardening her tone.

"Oh, no!" groaned Agnes. "Look, Rose, dear, we were just gossiping is all. There's nothing to what we said!"

"Is that right?" Rose smoothly inquired as she moved to a mirror hanging above a sink. Looking at her reflection, she snatched a tissue from a box and dabbed at her fire-engine red lipstick that went perfectly with her silver gown. She faced the women, crossed her arms and leaned against the sink. "If that's true then you'll have no qualms filling me in. I demand you tell me, or I swear on my mother's grave to make a scene, and I'll implicate the two of you as the reason for it."

Velma sighed. "We may as well let her know about the inheritance, Agnes."

"Inheritance?" Rose said.

"Once Jack marries, no matter whom he marries, he'll acquire his paternal Grandmother's estate and monies, which are substantial. But we're sure that's not the reason he's marrying you, Rose. Truly! You heard us talking about how he looks at you."

Rose's hands trembled as she clasped them in front of her, tried stilling them. Money was Jack's reason for wanting to marry her, and quickly. But why when the ground thaws a voice inside her asked.

"Why does he want to marry when the ground thaws?" *Of all things.*

"Because he's going into the house-building business and can't dig foundations until then," Miriam replied.

Rose understood now why he'd need an inheritance to pursue his business. Real estate property and lumber were expensive. Somehow, she'd always known Jack wasn't destined to be a bank accountant his entire life. He'd been educated and had acquired a degree in architecture, she knew, so it didn't surprise her to know he'd want to build homes. Especially now. Since the war had ended there was a decided shortage of available housing for the soldiers and their families.

Rose turned to look at her reflection in the mirror again, hating the tears building in her eyes. She dabbed at her eyes with the tissue then tossed it in the garbage can. Straightening her shoulders she said, "Thanks for your honesty. I appreciate it, especially since I was on the verge of making the biggest mistake of my life."

Rose took two strides when the Agnes and Velma closed in on her.

"No, wait!" shouted Velma. "You can't mean what I think you mean! Jack will be heartbroken if you break off your engagement."

A tear slipped from Rose's eye and she glared at Velma. "Who's the one with a broken heart? Jack Campbell and his broken heart can go to Hades for all I care."

Rose left with as much dignity as she could muster. Sweeping up her long skirts she headed out the door. She reached the coat check without running into Jack or anyone else she knew, which was a good thing since tears were now flowing freely down her cheeks.

The coat check attendant handed Rose her coat and said, "It's five minutes to midnight. Are you sure you want to leave now?" When Rose didn't reply but shrugged into her coat, the woman added, "Are you okay, miss?"

Rose raised her eyes, noted the worried look in the young woman's eyes. "I'll be fine as soon as I get out of here." She left then, made her way down the flight of stairs leading to the street, picking her way carefully over the snow in her silver heels.

Her head pounded with the onset of a migraine and just as she hailed a taxi and he stopped in front of her she heard Jack call out to her.

She paused with her hand on the taxi's open door and looked up at the top of the stairs. Jack stood there looking devastatingly handsome in his tuxedo, white shirt and bowtie. His black hair was still neat and tidy, and shiny from the pomade he'd used.

"Don't go, Rose. Let me explain," he begged.

Rose shook her head and shouted, "There's nothing to explain, you big lug! Just leave me alone!" She tucked herself into the taxi and said to the driver, "Please, leave now!"

The older man did exactly as Rose asked. She was astonished though, when she looked out her window and caught a glimpse of Jack running just to her left, nearly catching up to them.

"Faster!" she encouraged the driver.

"Lady, you want me to call a copper or something?" the driver asked.

"No. Just drive faster."

Half an hour later, Rose paid Sue Ellen, and chatted with the girl until her ride showed up. Rose stood outside, watched Sue Ellen and her father depart in their automobile just as a blue Studebaker came speeding up the street. Rose gasped, knowing immediately it was Jack and she rushed inside, slammed and locked her door.

Thankfully, she'd turned out all but one light earlier and she turned that one off too and stood against the front door, praying he'd leave if she didn't open the door. She couldn't talk to him now. She couldn't listen to his excuses, for that's what they'd be, nothing more. She couldn't, wouldn't allow him to damage her heart any more than he'd already done. And to think she'd allowed him to make love to her, and without a condom. By the time she remembered he'd already come inside her. It hadn't seemed to matter to him at all since, as he said, they were getting married and planned on having more children anyway.

She gasped when something pounded against the door, then the doorbell rang, and rang. "I know you're awake, Rose, so let me in!" Jack shouted.

Blast the man! She realized she'd have to talk to him otherwise he'd wake the entire neighborhood. But in one last ditch effort she hissed through the door, "Go away!"

"Not on your life, sweetheart. Let me in. I can explain everything. I love you."

"If you loved me," she choked out, "you would have told me the truth from the beginning. That you needed a marriage of convenience. I may have consented."

"No, you wouldn't have, and you know it. You're the most romantically-notioned woman I've ever met, Rose Delaney. You wouldn't have understood, and you wouldn't have accepted, even though gaining the inheritance is second to the fact that I love you with my entire being."

"I don't believe you," she said, sniffling. "How can I?" she asked, her voice breaking.

"Let me prove it to you."

"You can't."

"I can! I need you, Rose," he said softly.

Was that trembling in his voice she heard? No, it couldn't be. Jack Campbell didn't need anyone. He was an extremely self-sufficient man, and now she realized, for the first time, she needed a man who needed her. Jack Campbell did not need her. *But what about the money?* Well, it was true he needed her for that, but then, he could marry anyone to gain his darn inheritance.

"I'll call the police if you don't go away," she said as she hardened her heart and her voice.

All was silent for a while and she thought he'd left when he spoke again. She jumped, startled when he said coolly, his voice deep and harsh, "Don't expect me to give up on you. I won't."

She heard him swear beneath his breath. "You are behaving like a little girl—one that needs a firm hand. I'll leave, for now, but know that you'll be seeing and feeling my hand on your butt soon," he warned.

Rose gasped at his words. After a few moments she flung open the door, angrier than she'd ever been in her life, ready to flay him with words when she saw he'd left. She slammed the door shut, flinching at the sound and realizing too late the noise could wake Sarah.

She leaned back against the door as tears streamed down her face. She huddled her body with her arms and slid to the floor, her gown pooling around her as she sobbed late into the night.

Rose woke to a sunny but cold Sunday morning and groaned as she held her head in her hands and sat on the side of her bed. She'd stayed awake sobbing quietly in her lonely bed, into the middle of the night, unable to fall asleep in her despair. As she stood up she realized she'd finally fallen asleep in her gown and she groaned again, worried the wrinkles would never fall out, so crumpled was it.

She glanced at her clock sitting on the bedside table beside her and saw that it was ten o'clock. Darn it! Anger seeped into her again; anger toward Jack Campbell as he'd caused her to oversleep. Now she and Sarah wouldn't make it to church on time.

Rose decided a nice long soak in her bathtub was what she needed to start the day so she ran a tub full of bath bubbles, rose-scented, and soaked until the pads on her toes and fingers wrinkled. Then she'd dressed in a comfortable knee-length brown-tweed skirt and pumpkin-colored sweater that brightened her spirits somewhat. As she made her way slowly down the hallway she heard Sarah's chattering. Was she speaking to someone on the phone, she wondered?

She rounded the corner and came to a jarring halt at the sight of Jack sitting comfortably on her sofa, one leg crossed at the knee over the other, drinking a cup of coffee and talking with Sarah who sat beside him, an adoring look on her face.

Simultaneously, the two of them looked up at her as she stood in the archway.

Between gritted teeth, she said to Sarah, "Have you forgotten the rules about never opening the door to strangers?"

Sarah's eyes widened innocently. "Why, Mommy, Jack's not a stranger. You're going to marry him, remember?" She grinned and turned to Jack. "I've wanted a daddy forever!"

Rose's throat constricted, having forgotten that Sarah had been so excited about the two of them marrying she'd likely break the poor child's heart telling her the marriage was off. But there was really nothing else she could do.

"Sarah. We need to have a little talk, once Mr. Campbell leaves."

Jack frowned as he came to his feet. "No, we need to have a little talk first." He shook his head and added, "I can't believe you ran out on me last night the way you did."

Rose saw Sarah's eyes widen. "Did you have a fight with Jack at the party?"

Rose sighed. "Guess you could say that. Would you please go upstairs and watch television a bit while Jack and I have a discussion?"

Sarah looked between the two of them and said, "Okay, Mommy."

After Sarah left, Jack accused, "You've confused your daughter, and now you've upset her, besides."

"Don't you dare put any of the blame on my shoulders!

How dare you show up at my house, unannounced, and barge inside while I was asleep."

"I didn't barge in. Your daughter very civilly allowed me in. You've a lot to learn from Sarah." He settled himself on her sofa once more and stretched his arms out across the back on either side of him, a self-righteous expression on his face.

Rose couldn't control her anger any longer. She strode into the living room and came to an abrupt halt directly in front of him. She pulled her arm back, her intentions to make connection with his cheek when he caught her wrist and wrestled her down to his lap.

She struggled for release, but he held her fast. "Easy, easy now," he said softly. "You're going to listen to me once and for all. And then, if we don't come to some agreement, you can slap me. Agreed?"

"And if I don't feel like listening?" she blustered.

"Then I'll turn you over my knee and convince you," he growled.

Rose stared into his eyes, saw his sincere expression and gave a curt nod as she bit her lip. Once he released her she rose and sank into the chair across from him. There she folded her arms and waited.

"I liked it better when you were sitting on my lap."

"Too bad. Let's hear it, buster."

Jack grimaced. "You're not going to make this easy on me, are you?"

"Why should I? Why should I believe anything you say?"

Jack leaned forward, placed his elbows on his thighs and clasped his hands as he stared deep into her eyes. "Because you know, deep down inside, that I do love you. That the money doesn't make a darned bit of difference about how I feel. Admit it."

She shook her head. "I don't believe you, and I don't love you."

"You already told me you love me. I never thought you'd be the kind of woman who'd lie."

Grimacing at the disappointment in his voice she grudgingly said, "I'm not."

He sighed and said, "Let me explain."

She nodded again and waited, stilling her impatience.

He told her of his plans and how he required the money to buy the land for development. Explained how he'd be the housing contractor but that he'd have to pay salaries for carpenters to build his houses, which he'd turn around and sell, hopefully for a decent profit.

"So, you see, even if I don't secure the money, one way or another, I'll find a way to get it to start up this business. It's in my blood. I've dreamed of this for years and the dream hasn't changed. And I'll tell you something else, and you can verify it with my doctor; I planned on finding a woman to marry as soon as I could, but not because of the money, but because of the years of hell I'd endured during the war. Life is too precious, I learned, too short. I also need a wife to provide me with children to carry on my legacy.

"I'm thirty years old, Rose, and more than ready to be married, but not to just anyone, only you. Believe me when I say my love for you is true and will grow even more with the years we share together."

Rose tilted her head and gave him a long, considering look before saying, "Other than the children I could give you, why do you love me? Why do you need me?"

He frowned and straightened up on the sofa. "Well, now, that's a strange question."

She shook her head. "Not strange at all to my way of thinking. People bring certain things to marriage, aside from love and desire for each other and because of their desire for children. What do you need?"

It took him a long while to answer and when he did, Rose wasn't a bit surprised. "I think the love I feel for you, and the desire to be a father to any children we conceive is need enough, isn't it?"

"What about caring, friendship, and companionship?" she said.

"I feel all those things for you. You know I do."

She shook her head. "No, I don't know that."

His dark eyes pierced hers. "What do I have to do or say to convince you of my love?"

"Not a word," she choked out. "Only by deeds would I believe you. So far you've offered me nothing but frivolous words. Now I'd like you to leave."

He rose when she did. Then he reached out to take her hand, but she pulled it away from him. He sighed. "Call me when you realize you've made a mistake about me."

"Pardon me!" she exclaimed. "You're the one who needs to prove to me what you're made of."

"And you need to grow up," Jack growled, then left, slamming the door behind him.

Rose heard a cry and turned to find Sarah watching her, tears streaming down her cheeks. "Does this mean I'm not going to have a daddy?"

CHAPTER 11

Monday morning arrived, cold and blustery the sixth day of January 1947. Rose readied Sarah for the day then waited in her neighbor's driveway for her ride to school. Through the window Rose saw her daughter's scowling visage. Sighing, she watched and waved until she disappeared around the corner in Barb's car. Inside the house, Rose bathed and dressed in a red and brown plaid wool skirt and red sweater then sat down with coffee and toast and thumbed through the classifieds for jobs, all the while thinking about Sarah's disappointment. She'd just have to wait a while longer for a daddy.

Shortly after eight-thirty her telephone rang. "Hello?" she said, picking it up after the second ring.

"Why aren't you at work?" Jack's gruff voice sounded.

Rose was stunned and surprised to hear from him.

"Rose, don't you dare hang up on me!" he bellowed.

She jammed the receiver against her ear. "I quit, that's why I'm not there. As we speak, I'm looking through the job ads."

"Like hell you quit. You can't leave me high and dry like

this. You owe me a two-week notice. Now I'm advising you to get your fine little keister in here."

Rose couldn't help the laughter bubbling up from deep inside her. Never had she heard Jack be quite so crass. Internal laughter caused tears to slide from her eyes. Her voice quivered when she said, "You're absolutely right. In all fairness, I do owe you two weeks to find a replacement. I'll get there as soon as I can."

"I'll pick you up in half an hour."

"No! I'll take the streetcar, thank you," she said, her voice sounding ridiculously formal even to her own ears.

"Suit yourself," he growled.

She hung up the telephone then tore down the hallway to get dressed for work, all the while wondering why she was giving him notice when he'd lied to her. As far as she was concerned she didn't owe him that courtesy. *Because deep down inside you, you fool, you believe him!*

No! She wasn't going to cave into his charm and coercion. If he truly loved her he'd prove it in some important way, how or what, she had no idea. It was for him to determine the means and for her to then decide if what he decided was true and meaningful.

Rose arrived at the bank an hour later and stopped dead in her tracks after entering the office. An enormous bouquet of red roses in an exquisite crystal vase stood smack in the middle of her desk. A small gold-foil card stood in front of it. She admired the flowers, the aromatic scent flowing around her. Her hand trembled when she picked up the card and read the words inside, simply 'For You, Darling'. Love, Jack.

She moved around her desk and sank into her chair thankful Jack didn't seem to be anywhere around at the moment to see her happy expression. Her happiness dissipated then as she thought flowers were beautiful but to her mind it wasn't enough. Inside her, a small voice said, he would *have to prove his love in a true and meaningful way—and disprove the fact he wants marriage to her because of a stupid inheritance.*

Fortunately, Rose was answering a phone call when Jack appeared. He met her eyes a moment, swept an appreciative look over her before striding into his office.

By quitting time at five o'clock Rose was a bumbling mass of nerves, having often caught, throughout the day, Jack's unnerving hot eyed expression. He'd been courteous, inordinately polite and impersonal toward her. He seemed cool and in perfect control while she was fast losing hers. This didn't sit well with her at all and she made a quick escape while he was on the telephone.

Luckily, her streetcar arrived just as Jack was leaving the bank. She caught his frustrated expression as the streetcar passed by him. Satisfaction soared through her. His bribery, by way of the most gorgeous bouquet of flowers she'd ever received, and his polite manners hadn't worked. Pride filled her then that she'd managed to maintain control of her feelings for him. She had just had nine more days to endure his attentions.

She frowned and thought, so, why wasn't she happy about her short time left to work for him? And why did she feel as though her heart were breaking at the very idea of not seeing him again?

Rose knew the answer even though she tried to deny it; she loved him, which was why his betrayal had struck her so hard.

The rest of the week sped by quickly, but, by the end of that week, Sarah knew something was truly wrong between Rose and Jack. She confronted her mother on Saturday evening, as they sat side by side on the sofa and ate popcorn, playing a game of Monopoly.

"Mommy? I haven't seen Jack in a long time."

Rose sighed. "Haven't I explained it's not polite to address an adult by his or her first name?"

"Yes, but Jack said I could. When I call him Mister, he says he thinks I'm talking to his daddy!"

Rose set down her game piece. Truth telling could be so hard, but she had to tell her daughter, now that she'd finally asked. Frankly, Rose was surprised she hadn't asked earlier, though she had witnessed their fight.

"Jack is very busy, sweetheart. He's finishing up his work at the bank and is in the process of starting up his own business so he has little time to socialize, I'd imagine."

"Uh, when are you marrying him?"

Rose straightened in her chair at the kitchen table and looked directly into her daughter's eyes. "We've decided now isn't the right time for us to marry."

Sarah's wide-eyed expression changed. Her eyes narrowed, her lips pouted, and her spine straightened.

"So, when?" she persisted.

"I don't know," Rose replied as she picked up her game piece again. "Don't worry about us, honey. We've just hit a rut in the road. Things will smooth out soon."

That seemed to satisfy Sarah though guilt permeated Rose. She knew she'd merely pacified her daughter, leaving the door open to the possibility of her getting back together with Jack, when it wasn't likely.

The next week sped by and soon Rose was collecting her last paycheck. As she pulled on her coat, Jack assisted her. He smoothed down her collar and stared into her eyes.

"You haven't changed your mind about leaving?"

Rose tilted back her head, met his serious expression with a gentle smile. "No, I'm afraid not. I'd like us to remain friends, though. Sarah misses you."

Jack scowled. "Sarah does? How about you?"

Heat seeped into Rose's face as he continued to stare down at. "Don't push me on this."

"Push you!" he blurted out. "Damn it, Rose, I can't recall when I slept the entire night through without waking and thinking about you. You plague me in my sleep, in my dreams. Don't you even think about me one bit?"

His voice sounded injured. Rose's hands shook as she clasped them together. Oh, how she wanted to tell him how much she missed him, but she couldn't. He hadn't proved his love—his need—for her, except for the pretty words that slid easily from his lips.

She worried her lower lip a moment before saying, "I think of you often, too. But my feelings toward you haven't changed. Good night and good luck with your business venture."

Rose left quickly not wanting him to see her tears. She stood at her stop waiting for the streetcar to take her home as snow fell from the cloudy sky, blanketing the bushes and sidewalk. Someone got on a streetcar that arrived—not hers, unfortunately, and Rose sat on the bench to wait beside another woman. They chatted as they waited for the next streetcar, until it appeared. Just as Rose came to her feet she saw a blue Studebaker speed by, but not before she caught Jack's angry face in profile. Her heart clenched as she realized he hadn't looked her way.

❄

April 1947

Jack sat at O'Reilley's Pub, raised his beer mug to his friend, Greg Saylor. "Congratulations, partner."

Greg, Jack's best buddy from high school, tapped his mug against Jack's. "To us and to our future success!"

"Amen," Jack replied then swallowed down half his mug of beer. He swiped his hand across his lips and added, "And we did it without Grandma's money. Gee, but we're a couple of big cheeses, aren't we?"

Greg grinned. "You can say that again! Your mom's

something else, coming up with the money to help us out, but I don't think your dad was too happy about it."

"It's money she planned on giving me sometime soon, anyway, but she'd never told me about it. Dad knew, of course, but hadn't expected her to just hand it over to me, mostly because she's always done exactly as he's wanted, but not this time." Jack laughed. "If you could have seen the look on the old man's face. It was swell."

"Digging starts tomorrow, right?" Greg said.

Jack nodded. "Now that the ground's finally thawed. I was beginning to think winter would never end. It won't take long to build the spec house—about three weeks or so to excavate, build the foundation and the exterior walls, and roof it. We're a little behind schedule, but that's okay. I've already got folks interested in purchasing lots and building houses without a one of them having seen a house plan yet."

"Yeah, well, I can understand that. How would you like to be a newlywed and living with your in-laws?"

Jack grimaced. "Sorry. I know it's been hard for you and Virginia living with her folks but not for much longer. You get the second house we build. If all goes according to schedule I figure by October you'll be moving into your new place."

"I'm counting on it." Casually, Greg added, "Heard anything from Rose?"

Jack sighed. "Not a word. She's got to be the most stubborn dame I've ever met. I called her several times over the past three months, but always got Sarah on the line."

"Thought she wanted to be friends?"

"Uh-huh. At least that's what she said, but she's been unavailable every time I called. Needless to say, she's avoiding me. I've been thinking a lot about what she said. Can I ask you something?"

"Sure! Shoot."

"I never told you all the reasons why she broke off our engagement."

"Wasn't it because she heard your cousins yappin' in the powder room on New Year's Eve about your inheritance money?"

"Yes, but there's more. She says I don't need her, except for getting a few kids from her."

"I'd say that's one of the usual reasons a guy gets married," Greg said. "You did tell her you loved her, didn't you?"

"Of course! But she wants to know why. Why? Doesn't that beat all? How in the heck does a guy explain himself?"

Greg shrugged. "Beats me."

"How did you tell Virginia?"

Gruffly, Greg said, "That's private, between me and the wife. I will tell you this, though, be sincere, level with her. Tell her after fighting in the war you realize life is too short to live it alone."

"I did tell her, maybe not in the same words, though. It seems being a lonely war-ravaged soldier isn't a good enough reason to marry her, either. According to her I could marry anyone if all I wanted was companionship."

"You'll figure it out eventually. Besides, there's no accounting for how a dame thinks."

Jack sighed. "Amen. How about another beer?"

Later that evening Jack sat in his apartment at his kitchen table and paged through the yellow pages of the local telephone directory. He jotted down several names and numbers, then closed the book. Hopefully, soon, he'd find the answers that would help him prove his love for Rose was true; that the ultimate result of what he planned would make her fall madly in love with him.

Then he said a silent prayer that Timothy Delaney was, in fact, deceased.

CHAPTER 12

$\mathbf{G}$*ood heavens!* Rose thought. It wasn't summer yet and already Mosley's apothecary shop was stifling hot. But then, it was unseasonably warm for May. The Memorial Day holiday weekend was coming up and she looked forward to having a few days off. She hated every moment of her new job—one she'd worked at during her teens.

She admitted she was more than a bit surprised that Larry Mosley had hired her, especially after she'd slapped his face all those years ago when he'd pinched her butt. Larry had been the eldest son of Larry Mosley Senior, the owner of the apothecary shop. Often, she and Larry would work the same shift together. He'd been annoying as a teenager, but he'd grown into an unbelievably nice man, with a wife and kids.

There was no doubt about it; Rose had fallen on hard times.

Shortly after fulfilling his two weeks' notice to LaSalle, Jack also left LaSalle Bank to start up his business. Rose had decided to stay on to whomever Mr. Jorgenson hired to replace Jack. She hadn't counted on Mr. Jorgenson wasting no time letting her go and hiring someone to fill her secretarial position and Jack's position as well, leaving her without a job.

Jorgenson hadn't even allowed her to apply for either position, explaining he'd given her an opportunity and she hadn't met his standards. Never had Rose felt such anger and humiliation. Oh, if she were a man she wouldn't have experienced such prejudice, she guessed.

The only job she'd been able to find was soda counter girl in the Apothecary Shop. Luckily, Larry Mosley Jr. had had no ill feelings about her and had hired her on the spot. The pay was steady but abysmally low. She still kept an eye out every day for other positions and prayed soon she'd find a better paying job.

She hadn't heard nor seen Jack in months. But she'd held off her inclination to call him, knowing he needed to make the next move. She loved him, there was no doubt in her mind about it, but he would have to need her for something in his life besides giving him children. That seemed to be the primary reasons he'd wanted to marry, not to mention securing his inheritance, which still stung.

She'd learned he'd started his construction business. This surprised her and she wondered how he'd managed to secure the money since he hadn't yet married, which meant he hadn't gotten his inheritance.

She heard the jingle of the bell over the door. Someone had arrived for early lunch. She looked up from the glass she was drying, and her heart stopped. Jack stood before her counter, accompanied by another man who appeared to be of about the same age.

"Rose?" he said, scowling, "What are you doing back there?"

She raised her chin and glared back at him. "Working, of course."

"But what about your job at LaSalle?"

"Mr. Jorgenson decided, upon your leaving, that I really wasn't qualified for the accounting position."

"What! I can't believe it. And the secretary job?"

"Same reason," she said, hating the bitter sound in her voice. She smoothed down the skirt of her cotton candy dress, the uniform of all wait staff at the apothecary shop and smiled at the tall, blonde-haired man beside Jack and stuck out her hand. "Hello. I'm Rose Delaney, Jack's former secretary."

Greg grinned and took her hand. "A pleasure to meet you, ma'am. I'm Jack's business partner, Greg Saylor."

Jack waved his hand negligently. "Come on. We're going back to LaSalle. Jorgenson promised me you could retain the secretary position."

Rose held her ground. "You couldn't pay me a million dollars to work for him. I don't know how I stood his horrid behavior and bad treatment toward me for as long as I did." *She knew why; she'd needed the job.*

"Did he hurt you, Rose? I swear he'll deal with me if he did," he snarled.

"No, just my pride." She sighed when a stream of people entered the shop. "I've got to get back to work. Excuse me."

She turned away, moved down the long counter to where people were seating themselves and whipped out her pencil and notepad to take their orders.

Jack and Greg took seats on stools and picked up menus. Soon Rose appeared in front of them and they ordered hamburgers loaded with onions, fries and chocolate malts.

Jack couldn't keep his eyes off Rose as she worked behind the counter, deftly preparing food. She seemed to be a natural in the kitchen, and he knew she'd fit into his kitchen very nicely. Not only did he want her in his kitchen, he wanted her in his bedroom again. He's only experienced her sweet feminine charms once and he wanted her again.

She was so sweet, so beautiful—the most feminine woman he'd ever met. And he planned on making her his bride. He wouldn't allow her to escape. Her fate was settled and soon she would be his. He'd find a way to make her see that he needed her very much in his life, more than she'd ever imagine possible.

But now, as he watched her shove a loose strand of curly hair into the bun at the nape of her neck, he thought of a new plan; one that would get poor Rose out of this job and closer to him.

He looked at Greg and smiled. "Hey, aren't we going to need a secretary? Someone to type and answer the telephone?"

Greg narrowed his eyes. "Eventually. When business really takes off. Who have you got in mind?"

Jack looked between Greg and Rose.

Greg groaned and slapped his forehead. "Do I really want to get caught in the middle of your lover's quarrel?"

"Oh, if only we were lovers," Jack said wistfully. "I'm hoping we will be, once I get a ring on her finger, but now I'm thinking I need to get Rose a lot closer to me in order to work at changing her mind about me. And get her out of this hellhole of a job. What do you say?"

"Hey, you're the boss," Greg said. "Got a question, though. What makes you think she'll accept the job?"

Right then Jack decided his lead carpenter, Rory Conrad, would field the phone calls from applicants. "We'll run the ad in the paper and use Rory's phone number for people to call to apply instead of using my phone number or yours."

"Let's wait another month or so, until the spec house is ready for us to set up our office. We really won't need a secretary before then," Greg said.

"True. I'll talk to Rory tomorrow about our plans."

"Yeah, but don't you think being deceitful will make her even madder?"

"It'll give me the time I need to try and talk sense into her. I hope. By the way, how do you handle your wife when you argue?"

"You really want to know?" Greg asked.

Jack noticed how Greg's face turned rosy red.

"What the heck, you're burning up. This I got to hear."

Greg looked around conspiratorially, then whispered, "I spank her."

Jack jerked back. "And she puts up with it and doesn't call the cops on you?"

"No cops. She knows better, besides, as much as she complains, she enjoys it. It reminds her I wear in the pants in the house."

"How do you know she likes it?" Jack raised his brow.

"Because we have the best sex afterwards."

"I don't know that I could do that," Jack said uncomfortably.

Dryly, Greg said, "You get angry enough with her it might just happen anyway." He shrugged. "Worth a try. Just one swat might change her attitude—just a little attitude adjustment is all I'm saying."

They finished their meal then left healthy tips for Rose. They saluted by way of a good-bye to her and she smiled and gave them a careless wave, her eyes riveted on Jack.

As they left, Greg said, "Okay, I saw the look. No problem. She'll benefit from that little adjustment."

"How do you know?" Jack asked, frowning.

"I saw her looking all starry eyed at you. She'll take it to heart."

"Hmm, I'll think about it," Jack said, unsure.

After Jack dropped Greg off at his home, he started whistling a song. The title of it eluded him, but it didn't matter. Soon Rose would be his secretary again. Heck, he'd make her his office manager, not just his secretary. Rory would make her a wage offer she couldn't resist. But most importantly Jack would have the results of his investigation in hand, which should further his cause, and convince her of his love. If he could only think of another reason, other than the valid ones he already had as to why he truly needed her in his life, he'd be on easy street.

June 1947

School had ended and now Rose was faced with finding childcare for her daughter, which would accommodate her temporary work schedule at the apothecary shop. Larry had initially put her on the day shift, which was ideal, but now they'd lost their latest teen-age worker because she'd gotten in the family way. Larry had interviews lined up but wouldn't be hiring anyone for about a week. This meant he'd cover mornings to early afternoons while Rose covered the counter from two until ten each night.

Poor Missy Elert! Her parents were sending her away to a home to have her baby. After delivering the baby, she'd give it up for adoption. Missy had been so depressed and scared lately, but she hadn't confided in Rose about her problem, as they didn't know each other well.

Larry had told her today about Missy's predicament. He'd been upset, ready to punch rich-kid Harvey Mills' nose when he learned he was the jerk who'd taken advantage of Missy.

"Uh, Larry, would your wife be able to baby-sit for me, do you think?"

Larry pulled at his collar. "I don't think she can, Rose. She's working full-time herself then taking care of our kids at night. It would be too much for her. Once we reach our goal in savings, she'll be able to stay home with the kids, something we both want."

"I understand." Rose sighed. "I'll have to call around, see if some of my neighbors can help out for the next couple weeks. But two weeks only, Larry," she warned. "I can't stay on permanent nights."

"Two weeks tops!" Larry said cheerfully.

Her new hours would start tomorrow afternoon. She rode the streetcar home, jumped off at her stop and made her way toward her house, stopping at her neighbor's house.

Sarah had been coming to Barb Bradford's house after school for a few hours for the entire school year. Now that school had ended, Barb had willingly taken Sarah for the summer months during the day hours Rose worked. Barb had said it was no hardship, especially since Sarah and Barb's daughter, Mary, were the same age and good friends.

Now Rose stood in the front hallway of the Templeton's home and hugged Sarah. "How was your day?"

"Great!" Sarah said.

Rose grinned at the happy tone in her daughter's voice.

"Can Mary come over tonight and play with me?"

"Sure." Rose met Barb's eyes. "Until seven, okay?"

Barb laughed. "Hey, you're doing me a big favor. Gee, I love summer with the longer hours of daylight, don't you?"

Rose joined her laughter. But her humor faded, and she said, "Barb, I've got a problem."

Barb tilted her head and said, "What's wrong?"

After explaining the next two weeks of a changed schedule, Barb said, "I can take Sarah on Mondays, Tuesdays and Wednesdays but not the other two days. Sorry, but my husband and I bowl on a league on Thursdays and we usually drop Mary off at my mother's. And Friday is our date night." She blushed. "I know, it sounds silly after ten years of marriage that we still do that, but—"

"It's not a bit silly!" Rose protested. "I appreciate the fact you can take her three of the nights. You've been a fantastic neighbor and friend."

By Tuesday, before Rose left for work at one-thirty in the afternoon, she still hadn't found anyone to care for Sarah on Thursdays and Fridays. There was nothing she could do but take Sarah to work with her. Larry wouldn't like it but too bad! She had no other options and she was, after all, doing him a favor.

The idea of calling Jack and asking for help occurred to her but she wasn't sure how receptive he'd be to it since he was not happy with her and she'd spoken with him little over the past few months.

Rose had just settled Sarah down to bed at ten o'clock on Wednesday evening when the telephone rang.

"Hello," Rose said, unable to prevent the depression in her voice.

"What's wrong?"

Rose frowned. "Jack? Is that you?"

"Who else would be calling you this late at night? Where have you been the last two evenings?"

She explained her job situation to him, and her childcare problem. Jack surprised her when he said, "I'll leave work early those days and just stay at your place until you get home each evening."

"Oh! I couldn't impose on you that way."

"Yes, you can. And it's not an imposition."

"Well…"

"No hemming and hawing about it. It's only for four days."

"Thank you."

"It's the least I can do," he replied.

True, she thought. If it hadn't been for his inheritance, he guessed they'd still be together.

Rose felt heat sweep up her cheekbones at his comment and immediately felt guilty. "I owe you, Jack."

"You sure do, sweetheart. Does this mean you'll marry me after all?"

"Don't push your luck."

"Thought you might have changed your mind."

"Have you thought of a good reason or two why you need me in your life?"

"I've given you good reasons."

"In your opinion, you mean," she snapped.

"I didn't call to pick a fight," he said softly.

"So why did you call then?"

"Just to see how you and Sarah were doing."

Guilt settled over her then as she thought how she'd been dodging his telephone calls. Perhaps the man had truly meant what he said. Perhaps he *did* love her; maybe it was time to give him another chance to prove himself, but she wouldn't tell him yet.

How she wanted him back in her life again! She'd never wanted him out of it, but her feelings had been hurt when she'd learned about his inheritance. But she was beginning to believe she'd made a mistake for, in this crises moment, he was ready to help her. Wryly, she thought how she'd needed him, but she'd yet to hear his reasons for why he might need her, aside from acquiring his darned inheritance.

CHAPTER 13

Timothy Delaney peered cautiously over the edge of the newspaper he'd splayed out in front of him. Damn! The guy was still there. Slowly, he raised it once more, concealing his eyes. The guy's small, beady eyes pierced Timothy, lasering right through the newsprint. He realized now his suspicions were true. He was being followed. After spotting the guy for the third time he knew it was true. What in the hell did he want with him, anyway?

Maybe he should confront the guy, once and for all. But he had a feeling he was a pro and wouldn't divulge an iota of information. And from what Timothy had seen of him over the past week, the guy would probably plaster him if he did confront him. But why was he being followed and investigated?

He peered out his window and saw his stop was coming up. He quickly folded the paper, tucked it under his arm, reached up and pulled the cord, warning the streetcar driver he would be leaving.

His legs shook when he stood, brushed by the man, then tore out of the streetcar. Relief flooded him when the guy hadn't exited the streetcar right behind him. But as he walked down the street toward his and Margaret's apartment he flicked a quick look over his shoulder and his heart started racing. The man had left the streetcar a block later and was following him.

Timothy's gait was long and quick as he drew near the apartment. Instead of entering the front door he tore around to the back side of the red brick, three-story building and ducked inside the back door.

Through the one lone hallway window, covered with a tacky turquoise-colored café-style curtain, he peered between the panels. The man had followed him but paused on the sidewalk, stared down the alley. He started heading quickly down the alley but slowed, then paused, stopping altogether.

He fell to his knees and peered out the window, from between a split in the curtain. At that moment, the guy whirled around and, once again, stared toward the window. Timothy knew he couldn't see him still he shuddered at the man's beady-eyed fierce expression.

"Rory, think you can conduct the interview without letting on to Rose that I'm the owner of Grand Horizon Homes?" Jack asked.

Rory smiled. "Sure. And if she asks I'll just tell her the truth; that I'm one of the partners and hope she doesn't ask the name of the other."

"If she does, you won't have any choice but to be honest," Jack replied.

"I'll steer her away from the conversation best I can," Rory said. He rose, pulled his enormous bulk from the chair and shook Jack's hand.

After Rory left, Jack thought about his new business venture. In three weeks' time Jack's crew had built the spec house and Jack had made one of the bedrooms into an office.

The interior designer he'd hired was currently working in the kitchen and living areas of the house with swatches of fabric, linoleum and carpeting, deciding upon a color scheme. Eventually, the house would be sold, but for now it was office space for the business.

Jack was also ready to hire himself a secretary, and the only one that would do was Rose. He hoped, once she accepted the job and discovered he was the owner of Grand Horizon Homes, she wouldn't be too steamed at him and quit. Now that most of the soldiers had returned from active duty, there was a shortage of both housing and jobs for widows like Rose who needed to work. If she didn't accept the secretarial job he'd up the position to office manager at a higher salary and see if she'd bite.

He didn't think she'd quit once he hired her. Jack was in a position to pay her well; nearly as much as she'd earned working at the bank in his accounting position. Hopefully, too, she'd listen to him and accept the truth of the matter; that he loved her, and it was okay for her to need him. Contrary to what she believed, it wasn't important that he need her, with the exception of becoming his sweet, loving wife and mother to his children. It would be enough.

But also, once he heard back from Ryan Grahams, the P.I. he'd hired, on the status of Rose's husband, Timothy, the fact he'd gone to such depths to find him should tell Rose how much Jack cared for her he assumed.

Word had gotten around town about the new housing development and the telephone rang frequently. Jack couldn't afford to lose a single customer, and if he had to leave the office that meant no one would be there to answer the phone. He'd already placed the ad to hire a secretary in the newspaper and soon the phone would be ringing with people asking to apply. The only one that mattered was Rose. He hoped she still scanned the ads on a daily basis and would see the posted position and apply for it. He didn't know what he'd do if she didn't.

One week later, Jack sat behind his desk, knowing his expression was morose. Rory and Greg had received nearly a hundred applications, though he had no intention of hiring any of them. But the one application he hadn't received yet was from Rose. Could she have missed the ad, he wondered? Or, maybe she'd stopped looking completely for a job since she hadn't had any luck previously.

But his glum feelings weren't due only to Rose not applying for the job, but for another

Jack had also learned Timothy Delaney, the jerk, had married another woman, even though he was still legally married to Rose. Could he have been injured in the war and hadn't recalled his marriage? Maybe. Jack knew he had to tell Rose, but how would he explain why he'd hired the investigator to find Delaney in the first place? He'd convince her this more than proves his love for her, which was the reason, and to his mind it was a good one; he wanted Rose free and clear from any past relationships.

After a few moments pondering he knew he'd have to tell her the truth; that he'd wanted to rid them of anything, or anyone, that could keep them apart. Rose would believe that for he knew deep down inside she believed he truly did love her. He'd gone the whole mile, and more, to try and settle things between them by finding Delaney. The problem was he knew how devastating this news would be for Rose; knew she didn't believe in divorce, but she'd have no other recourse since Delaney had already married another woman.

He finished the bologna and cheese sandwich he'd smacked together carelessly between two pieces of white bread that morning, wishing he had a wife to cook him a nice meal on Sunday evening, then send him off with leftovers Monday morning.

Today was the last day the ad would run in the

newspapers. As he tried to decide if he should run it another week or not the phone rang. He started to reach for it then remembered it wouldn't do any good if this was Rose calling and she recognized his voice. He looked up and sighed, relieved when Rory tore into the office.

Rory leaned across Jack's desk and tore the phone off the hook. "Grand Horizon Homes!"

As Rory wrote on a pad of paper Jack saw a slow grin cross his lips. After he hung up he looked directly at Jack. "Bingo."

Jack hooted then said, "I'll call the other applicants to let them know we hired someone else for the job."

By noon the following day Rory had conducted the interview with Rose and had made her a generous offer of employment. Eagerly, she accepted. The only disappointment was the fact Rose had been compelled to give a two-week notice to the apothecary shop.

But now, as Jack leaned back in his desk chair, his ankles crossed, feet upon his desk, he smiled in satisfaction. Life was good and would be even better in two weeks when Rose started working for him. But he frowned when he thought about how angry she might be once she discovered he owned the company. He could, of course, tell her that Rory had had no idea they'd known each other before, but guessed she wouldn't believe him. After all, since Rory was not only his employee but a very good friend, wouldn't he have discussed her qualifications with him before making her an offer?

He shrugged off his worries, deciding he'd tackle the problem if it arose.

That evening, as he sat in the living room in his apartment listening to the radio, his telephone rang. He picked it up on the second ring and heard an excited, breathy, decidedly female voice.

"Jack? You won't believe this, but I landed the best job ever!"

Jack frowned. "Rose. I, well, I'm glad for you." Guilt seared his conscience as he tried to decide how to show his happiness for her, praying she wouldn't divulge the company name because then he'd need to tell her the truth.

"Thanks. It's only a secretary position but it pays nearly the same as the accounting job at LaSalle. Can you believe it?"

"Sure I can. You're a talented woman. You deserve the job."

"Mommy? Can I talk to Jack?"

Jack breathed a sigh of relief when Rose replied, "May I, you mean."

"May I?" Sarah parroted.

"Sure, honey. Uh, Jack, Sarah would like to speak to you."

"Sure thing."

"Jack?" Sarah said. "When can you come over? I got some new card tricks to show you!"

He chuckled. "Whenever your mom says it's okay, sweet-cakes."

He heard murmuring in the background then Sarah's voice blaring into the telephone.

"Mommy said you can come over anytime. What about now?"

Jack checked his watch, saw it was nine o'clock. "It's too late, but how about tomorrow after supper?"

More discussion ensued before Sarah returned. "Mommy said that's fine."

"Okay," Jack said. "I'll be by around 6:30."

The following day he arrived on Rose's doorstep by 6:15. Sarah answered the door then, with a little shriek of joy, flung herself against Jack's knees and held on tight.

"Hey, hey," he said, patting her hair, "what a welcome."

She held onto his legs and grinned up at him. "I haven't seen you for so long!"

"Hey, it was just three weeks ago when I watched you

when your mom was working those crazy hours," he said and gently, fingering her hair.

"Oh! Mom is so happy cause she got a new job!"

She released him and dragged him inside, slamming the door behind them. In the living room she plopped down on a pillow she'd positioned before the coffee table and proceeded to line up her playing cards in a particular pattern.

"Remember I told you I learned some new tricks?"

"Yes, I remember," he said as he sank down to the sofa behind her.

"Well, I'd better start showin' them to you now since I learned a whole bunch!"

Jack chuckled and shook his head. "Darlin', I've got all night."

Just then Rose entered the living room and Jack's heart skipped a beat. How in the heck could one woman be so beautiful, he wondered?

His gaze swept over her and after a moment he frowned. He couldn't believe his eyes—couldn't believe what Rose wore.

"What do you think, Captain Jack?" she said.

Jack was tongue-tied as he watched Rose pivot around and position her backside to him. She glanced at him over one shoulder, hands on her flaring hips and smiled at him.

He gulped as he took in her sweet butt encased in a tight pair of black slacks. Pants! On a woman? *Not his woman,* his mind blared, but then he pulled back on the reins. Wait a minute. She wasn't his woman yet. He tried to focus on her chattering rather than on her charming backside.

"This is the first pair of slacks I've ever owned. I love them! They're, well, they're just so liberating!"

Liberating? Somehow Jack didn't like that word. Not one bit.

"Uh, Rose, where I come from, at least in my family, the men wear the pants in the house."

Rose turned to Sarah and said, "Honey? Would you pour us some sodas?"

"Sure, Mommy!"

After Sarah scampered off to the kitchen Rose turned to Jack and said, "Stop being so stuffy. In this house the women wear pants. I am, after all, the head of this household."

"Yes, I know," he growled. "Now go change into one of those sweet little dresses you own, or a sweater and skirt."

She narrowed her eyes on him. "It's eighty degrees in the shade. I put up all of my winter clothes in the cedar closet."

Now he narrowed his eyes on her as he gathered his thoughts and his words before replying. After a moment he said, "I just happen to think women's bodies were meant for dresses, not pants." *Liar!* The little voice inside him blared. *She looks real swell in pants.*

Rose shrugged. "It doesn't matter what you think. We're not seeing each other, after all."

Jack tugged at his shirt collar. "Yes, well, I'd like to change that. As a matter of fact, that's why I came over."

"Oh?" she asked, raising her brow. "I thought it was because you were congratulating me on the new job. And Sarah wanted to show you card tricks."

"Those too, but primarily it's to ask you out to dinner and a show."

"A show?"

"Yes, you know, as in movie show?"

She sighed and smiled faintly. "I haven't seen a show in years."

Jack frowned. "Why not? You live within spitting distance of two theaters."

"One very good reason—no extra money."

"I've got plenty of that so how about it? Supper at the Commodore Hotel dining room then onto the Plaza?"

"What's showing?"

"Anchor's Away."

Rose clapped her hands. "Oh, wonderful! I love watching Gene Kelly tap-dance. He's so talented and I've heard the music is wonderful, too!"

"Then it's a date?"

She paused, bit her lip and watched him from beneath lowered eyelashes then said, "Yes, I'll go, if I can find a sitter."

Jack grinned. "Great."

"Mommy? I need help," Sarah whined from the kitchen.

Rose gave Jack an apologetic smile. "I'll be right back."

Rose returned balancing a tray with three ice-filled glasses and two bottles of Cola, Sarah bouncing happily along at her side. She set the tray down carefully on the coffee table and proceeded to pour the beverage into the glasses.

Rose passed a glass to Sarah and Jack. She watched Jack take a couple of long pulls.

"Ah, that's wonderful," he said with a smile. "I was thirsty." Then he looked at Sarah. "How about showing me more of those card tricks?"

CHAPTER 14

July 1947

Monday morning, Rory was in the office at Grand Horizon Homes when Rose arrived for work. Her work location was in a northern suburb of St. Paul, and very few streetcars went there so she was half an hour early. But better early than late, she mused.

She wore a lightweight, seersucker blue and white striped suit composed of a suit jacket and narrow skirt with white high heeled shoes. She wanted to look her best her first day on the job.

"Mrs. Delaney," Rory said, "welcome to Grand Horizon Homes."

She shook his hand. "Thanks for having me. I'm looking forward to working with you."

"There are, besides you and me, two others that work out of this office. When they arrive I'll introduce you to them."

"Wonderful," she said, excitement flaring through her. To have such a good paying job was super, she mused, even if her title was secretary and not accountant.

"To whom will I report?" she asked.

"You'll be the mainstay in the office since us other three are out and about meeting with new clients, working with banks on loans and such, so you report to all of. Sorry, all guys. This is the building industry, after all, so hope you don't mind. You will primarily be answering phones, setting up appointments, typing up housing contracts, and such."

"Sounds interesting and I promise I will do my best," she said.

Rory took her on the tour of the spec home as they called it, which was currently their office, pointing out all she'll need to know for the job, including how to work the latest typewriter.

Rose knew how to type, self-taught, so she was glad she'd learned. It turned out much of the home buyer contracts they'd be issuing she'd be typing each one individually, per client.

After eating her homemade lunch of bologna and cheese sandwich and an apple Rory took her on an outside tour. It was slow-going as she wore high heels which were difficult to navigate in over the rocky, sandy terrain of the construction site, but she toured two of the new houses and was impressed with the quality of the work.

Once they returned to the office, she had many questions. It was getting near the end of her workday and she hadn't met the other partners in the business she'd be working with yet as they hadn't arrived.

"Will the others be here today to meet them before I leave?"

"Tough to tell. They're all over the place drumming up business for us and keep an unpredictable schedule."

"Well, I'm sure I'll meet them soon."

"Oh, you will."

She watched him at his desk as he rummaged through paperwork, not meeting her eyes. She frowned. Had she asked too many personal questions?

As she finished up with a phone call she grabbed her purse, noted the time as 5:02 and readied to leave to walk the five blocks to catch the next streetcar when she heard a familiar voice followed by a decidedly familiar laugh.

She riveted her eyes on the doorway and she gasped when it opened and Jack Campbell walked in, followed by his friend Greg she'd met at the apothecary.

"Rose!" he said, hurrying toward her. "Glad you made it. How was your first day on the job?"

"What?" she asked, confused. "How do you know—what are you doing here?"

He grinned, removed his cream-colored fedora and tossed it on her desk. She noted he was dressed in a fawn-colored suit, with double-breasted jacket and pants, though it was 80 degrees outside he looked cool, crisp and comfortable, not to mention amazingly handsome. Upon her arrival to work she was surprised by how cool the house-office was, expecting it to be hot, but Rory explained about the air-conditioning. Oh, she'd love to have it in her own home, she mused.

"I work here too."

"Excuse me?" she said tightly. She was getting a very bad feeling about this.

"So does Greg. We're the owners of Grand Horizon Homes."

"You don't say?" she said softly as she slammed her desk drawer shut—hard.

"Yep, our new enterprise. When you told me you had a new job I had no idea—"

"Don't you dare fib," she snapped.

With her harsh statement she saw Greg and Rory disappear from the office and haul butt outside. She wasn't happy with them either.

He frowned. "Not lying about anything. We posted the job ad, you replied, and Rory interviewed and hired you. End of story."

"You knew I was looking for a higher paying job. And several others must have interviewed."

"We did, but Rory felt you would be best for the position."

"Did you know I'd applied?"

"Yes, he told me, and I gave him my opinion."

He sighed and sank down on top of her desk near her, blocking her way so she couldn't run out. Jamming his hands in his pockets, he said softly, "We need to talk. Come out to my car and I'll give you a ride home, darlin'."

"You—you lied to me," she whispered harshly.

"Don't make me out to be the bad guy here, Rose. I'm not."

She felt heat in her face, feeling like a fool that he'd played with her as he had. "I need this job," she said softly, and bit her lip.

❄

"It's yours, sweetheart," he said and rose to his feet. Reaching out to pull her into his arms she stepped around him, snatched up her purse from the desk and headed toward the doorway. "Stop right there," he ordered, steel in his voice.

She cut her hand through the air then whirled around to face him. He watched her open and dig in her purse for a handkerchief and dab at her eyes. This woman, what she did to him... He strode over to her and grasped her upper arms but didn't pull her close.

"I can't change the fact this is my company, and yes, I knew you'd applied, and I suggested we hire you. That's the extent of it. I didn't coerce you into applying, did I?"

Rose shook her head and looked down at the floor.

"Look at me," he coerced.

She shook her head and wouldn't. He placed a finger under her chin and raised it. "Rose," he began.

Her eyes flitted up to his and she said, "I just wished you'd told me you were hiring in your business, provided the name of it. Then I would have known not to respond to the ad."

"We were hardly on speaking terms, remember? Until you called and told me you had a job and Sarah invited me over. Besides, I just couldn't see you continuing to work behind that counter at the apothecary shop—work below your abilities. I just couldn't."

Rose nodded. "I do understand that," she said. "All right…" She stepped away from him. "You know my rules on no dating fellow employees. That still stands."

"If you insist."

"I do. Absolutely."

He could work with that, he decided, as much as he wasn't crazy about it. But he also knew he could wear her down. She was in love with him but had her pride. And he was in love with her. He'd convince her eventually. If only his P. I. would get back to him with a definitive answer on Timothy Delaney.

He backed away from her, sauntered back to her desk with his hands deep in his pants pockets.

She glanced down at her watch and sighed.

"Good night."

"You're coming back tomorrow, right?"

She nodded, left the office and started walking. After she'd walked across the construction site and onto the main road he got in his car and followed her, knowing she was walking to the nearest streetcar stop. He had no idea how far away it was, though.

Five blocks he soon learned, and he pulled up in front of the stop, leaned over and opened the passenger door. "Get in, sweetheart. I'm driving you home."

"I don't think so."

He gritted his teeth. "I said get in. Last time I'm offering."

She shook her head and stood in her white high heels, clutching her purse. Her shoulder length hair had started curling up from the heat and humidity, making her look like a little girl.

He got out of the car, stormed around to where she stood. "Last chance," he said softly. When she shook her head stubbornly he spanned his hands around her waist and easily hauled her up and over one shoulder. She was a real lightweight.

"What are you doing?" she protested. "You said it was the last offer!"

"Last offer before I *made* you get in the car."

"Just leave me," she spouted as she started kicking her feet. He began to lower her into the seat and he just couldn't help reacting and not thinking for he reached up and slapped her butt hard. Once in warning.

Immediately, she stilled as he lowered her into the passenger seat and slammed the door shut without another word. He got behind the wheel, started up the car and drove. He hadn't consciously meant to take Greg's advice—it just sorta happened.

After a long bout of silence and her looking out the window and not at him, he heard her soft words.

"You…you struck me," she accused.

His grip on the steering wheel tightened. "Once, just to get you to calm down. And if you ever ignore my trying to help you again, I'll do it again."

She glanced over at him with a scowl, then she sighed. "Sorry, you were only trying to help me out, like you said."

"Exactly. I've been trying to help you since day one of our meeting, but you just won't let me. You know how I feel about you, Rose. You know," he insisted. "Hell, we shared your bed and—"

"I…I do," she inserted.

"Then give us a chance!" he shouted.

"I just don't think it's a good idea for us to be dating and working together. You know how I feel about that."

"Make an exception—for us. Do it," he ordered.

"I'm still married. It was wrong of me to go on the few dates we had. Until I learn what happened to Timothy, my conscience won't allow me to date anyone. And never should I have agreed to marry you, Jack, since I am technically married."

He held his tongue, knowing now he had to get the last of the information on her husband sooner than later.

"Agreed," he said. "By the way, be ready by 9 tomorrow morning. I'm giving you a ride into work and taking you home every night."

"But—"

He shot a quick scowl at her. "Do you want me to show you again who wears the pants around here? Cause it sure as hell isn't you, sweetheart."

"No," she said softly, and she turned and looked out the window again, but not before he saw the red hue of her complexion.

He smiled to himself, sat up straighter, even though he couldn't get her to engage in any further conversation. Just as well, he mused, for he didn't want to get into another fight with her. But he had to admit she had a lovely behind, and that it might be worth getting into another argument. Like he told her, he wore the pants, and she might rule her roost at home, but she didn't with him.

Leaving his apartment the next morning for work at the Mobile Press Newspaper office, Timothy Delaney bumped into his stalker.

He'd had enough. He shoved the guy back a couple paces and snarled, "Why in the hell are you following me? Who are you?"

Paul Arends, the private investigator Jack Campbell had hired sighed. "You're Timothy Delaney."

"What of it?" he snarled in reply.

"Your wife is looking for you."

Timothy gave the guy a confused look. "What are you talking about? I just left my wife upstairs in our apartment. She knows I'm going to work."

"Not that wife."

CHAPTER 15

November 1947

F our months later, Jack got the call he'd been waiting for from Paul Arends.

"Found him."

Jack had picked up his phone, expecting another possible client to buy a house when he recognized Paul Arends, his private investigator's voice.

"You sure it's him?"

"Positive identification, based on the wedding picture of the two of them you provided and public records."

Jack sighed. "Damn, not the news I wanted to hear, but what's his excuse for leaving her behind?" He had to be careful as Rose was sitting at the desk on the opposite side of their office space. At a time like this he decided it was time he built himself an office with walls and a door he could close.

"Turns out the guy has had amnesia all these years. His memory never came back. He was in a hospital after being injured at Pearl Harbor. He ended up after a month's stay recuperating, then upon release marrying the nurse who took care of him. Needless to say, the guy's not faking it. I've talked to his doc."

"He's married?" Jack said louder than he should have.

"Yep, sure is."

"Damn, I'll get back to you. I need to do some thinking on this."

"Before you go, he wants to talk to wife #1 and see if she'll divorce him. He loves his current wife. He's sad about her having gone through a pregnancy and having a baby without him there, but he can't see any point in them being married. To him, he said, it'd be like marrying a stranger. He also said he doesn't want to meet the kid but is willing to pay child support—amount that he can afford."

"But since he doesn't want to meet the child and doesn't plan on being in her life, there's no point paying."

"Got it."

"Let me get back to you."

At five o'clock quitting time, Jack drove Rose home. He was quiet, thinking about Timothy and she must have noticed.

"You're awfully quiet today. Anything wrong?" she asked.

Shaking his head, he said, "No, just thinking over some house deals is all."

"Ah," was all she replied.

They arrived at her house and he gave her a quick peck on the cheek, then as soon as she got out of the car he sped away.

She stood there, following his rapid departure, thinking something just didn't feel right. After a long while she shrugged and went into the house, called Barb to let her know she was home for Sarah.

December 1947

"Say, Rose, do you have a minute?"

Rose looked at Rory and raised an eyebrow. "Of course."

"In private?" he added.

She looked around the office and for once everyone was there at the same time. "We'll have to go outside."

"Fine with me."

She felt Jack's eyes on her back as she led the way outside, first snatching her coat, hat and gloves from the closet.

"What's going on?" she asked, once Rory joined her.

He looked over his shoulder, through a window and squinted when he saw Jack watching them. Ducking his head, he smiled to himself.

"Listen, I know you have this rule about not dating guys from work, but I have a proposition for you. My date for the holiday ball we're throwing at the Convention Center fell through. I know you weren't going to go but I hate going to this kind of event stag. Would you come with me?"

She gave him a wide-eyed look. "You do know this will anger Jack, right?"

He grinned. "Sure do. You won't marry him if he doesn't give you good reasons. I'm thinking this might coerce him into give you some, other than the objectionable few he has already."

She bit her lower lip, thinking. Finally, she said, "Hmm, maybe this will help him think harder for other reasons, aside from gaining his inheritance and me being a broodmare for him."

"Exactly."

"Well, I guess it wouldn't do any harm to go as friends. And I was sort of wishing I'd bought a ticket and then the company ran out. Are you sure it'll be okay? Your girlfriend won't get upset?"

"Oh, she'll be upset because the food and drinks are super special that night of the event but she's an on-call nurse and she already knows now, a week ahead, that she has to work so can't attend."

Rose smiled. "Okay, then it's a date."

"Besides, I can't think of a better opportunity for Jack to have to examine his feelings about you. Can you?"

"Oh, I already know his feelings. He's waiting for me to cave and marry him."

"Then seeing us together should make him try harder, don't you think?"

"Hmm, when you put it that way, it makes me want to stay home."

"You mentioned you're waiting to hear his true feelings about you, right?"

She nodded briskly. "Absolutely."

Jack poked his head out the door. "You two are going to be ice cubes if you don't get your butt in here soon."

Rory saluted him. "Right, Captain. On our way."

That evening, Jack called her.

"What were you and Rory jawing about?" he inquired, point blank.

"Do you inform me of every conversation you have with people? I don't think so."

"So you're saying it's private."

"Just business is all," she said evasively.

"Uh-huh. Right. Later."

She frowned at the phone when he hung up on her.

The following Saturday evening, Rory showed up on her doorstep, dressed to the nines in a black tuxedo. He really was a handsome man and his girlfriend was one lucky gal, still she was happy he had that extra ticket. She wanted to get to know some of the other guests attending the event—mostly clients.

It had been almost a year since she'd attended any kind of party type event.

She dressed in the long silver gown, the one she'd worn to the holiday party sponsored by Jack's family last year.

The neckline was low and drapey, both in the front and back, exposing cleavage and almost her entire back. Sleeveless. She wore her pearl necklace and earrings and her one new purchase, a pair of elbow length white gloves. She also wore the silver heels from last year as well. Her hair had grown longer, and she wore it in an upswept style, showing off her long neck. She'd found a faux fur short jacket at a consignment shop and she grabbed it and her small clutch when she heard the doorbell ring.

"Mommy, I'll get it!"

"No, Sarah, stranger alert," she shouted running down the hallway. She stopped beside her daughter and saw Sarah's eyes go big and round as she stared up at the handsome Rory. Rory was Irish, tall, slim, black hair and deep blue eyes—a to die for handsome man. He was also a true Casanova and wondered how his girlfriend put up with him. Sarah was in love. She smiled, seeing her daughter stare at him.

"You're not Jack," she finally said softly.

"No, I'm not, but I'll bet you're Sarah."

She nodded but had no other words.

Sue Ellen the sitter showed up then and Rose and Rory left quickly.

They arrived at the Convention Center in downtown St. Paul and Rose gasped as they walked inside, admiring the holiday decorations.

"Place is something else, isn't it?" Rory said as he guided Rose to the coat check.

"I'll say," she murmured, admiring the almost ceiling high decorated Christmas trees, twinkling white lights throughout and creamy netting decorating the ceilings.

They moved into the ballroom where waiters held trays with hors d'oeuvres and champagne. Rory handed her a glass of bubbly and she plucked a shrimp toast off a tray as a waiter went by. Rory grabbed some of several. She laughed as he stuffed his mouth.

"Only reason I come to these events is 'cause I can eat for free."

"Well, paying $50 a ticket I wouldn't call free, Rory," she said. "Are you sure I can't reimburse you for the ticket?"

"No, absolutely not."

He looked over her head and said softly, "Oh-oh."

She saw his eyes widen. "What's the matter?"

"Jack. He doesn't look happy to see us together."

She sniffed. "Too bad."

"What in the hell," she heard Jack say softly under his breath as he stopped beside them.

He glared at Rose. "I asked you to come with me. You said you didn't have a sitter."

She shrugged. "Suddenly I was feeling the holiday spirit and found a sitter after all."

Jack sent a harsh look at Rory. "And where's Angela?"

Rory's girlfriend, Rose knew.

"She got called in last minute to work at the hospital so I invited Rose to come with me and use the ticket."

"I see," Jack said.

Rose thought she could see steam rising from his head but decided it was her imagination.

"Dance with me?" he said softly, turning to Rose, reaching for her arm.

She backed away and wound her arm through one of Rory's. "Not until I've at least danced once with Rory, my date."

Rory quickly set his plate and champagne glass down on a side table, followed by Rose's then led her out on the floor. He grinned down at her. "Did you happen to see the steam coming off Jack?"

"Oh, yes, most definitely steam," she said and laughed as they danced.

❄

Jack leaned against a wall, a highball in hand, glaring at Rose and Rory. What in the hell? He'd asked Rose to accompany him weeks ago when she reminded him she didn't date guys she worked with. So she has the nerve to show up with Rory. And Rory? What in the hell was he pulling anyway?

He'd find out when he got him backed into a corner this evening. It wasn't long before they returned from the dance floor and Jack swept her onto the dance floor.

Jack held her close, staring at her with steely eyes. He cleared his throat then to alleviate the silence. "You look beautiful, Rose."

She inclined her head and pushed a bit back from him, but he pulled her right back against him, tight to his chest. "You look beau—handsome," she murmured.

He shrugged. "Black tux like every guy here, but that silver dress—it looks familiar," he said, looking her over carefully.

"I wore it last Christmas to your family's event before the holidays."

"Ah yes, when you broke off our engagement."

"Yes, she said, how time flies. Hard to believe it happened a year ago," she murmured, unable to meet his eyes.

"Not to me," he groused. "Longest year of my life."

He slid his hand at her waist lower over her bare back revealed by the dress. She was fine with that but when he lowered his hand to her butt and pulled her tight against him, she reached back and moved his hand higher. He simply smiled down at her and moved it to her butt again.

Leaning over her when she went to move his hand up again, he whispered, "Don't. I don't think I need an excuse to spank you, showing up with Rory as you have—a guy with whom you work."

"You can't! You wouldn't," she exclaimed.

"Wouldn't I?" he inquired in a dangerous tone, tapping her nose. "You don't know how much I want to punish you for breaking your own rule, which makes me wonder why you did," he growled. "Maybe to make me notice—to make me jealous?"

"No!" she spat. "I was feeling bad that I would be sitting home, and the tickets were sold out by the time I could afford to buy one. Rory told me about the situation with Angela having to work. I didn't want to see him out $50 so I consented to go in her place."

"That was generous of Rory. Why when I asked you didn't you consent to come with me in the first place? I said I'd pay for your ticket and you refused."

She squeaked and stiffened when he pinched her butt before moving his hand up to her back again.

"Ouch," she complained.

"More where that's coming from. When you're my wife, you will obey me, Rose. Those are in the wedding vows. You know that."

"I told you we are not getting married, unless you can come up with reasons why—other than the two objectionable ones you've already given me, which won't suffice."

He just smiled at her and delivered her to the table where Rory and a few other clients were sitting. He bowed low over her hand and moved to the bar once more. He took a stool and nursed a brandy for a bit, lit a cigarette, took a couple drags, grimaced then put out the cigarette in an ashtray in front of him. Behind the bar was a continuous mirror and he positioned himself where he could watch Rose and Rory. After a while, he saw Rory come to his feet and leave the ballroom. He set down his drink and followed him out, thinking in a way how the other man was leading him somewhere particular. Which he was.

Jack met up with Rory in the outer area of the men's room. After they took care of business they stood side by side, fixing their bowties, looking in the mirror.

"What the hell, Rory," Jack finally said.

Rory burst into laughter. Jack glared at him until Rory got himself under control.

"This is not a funny situation," Jack said.

"Oh, yeah, buddy, it sure is," Rory retorted.

"Why?" Jack asked quietly.

"It's the only way I could think of to get you two together to talk."

Confused, Jack said, "What in the hell are you talking about?"

"Oh, didn't I tell you I have to leave? Angela got off of work early and she can't get her car started so I have to pick her up."

Jack gave Rory a piercing look that broke slowly into a big grin. "You rascal, you," he drawled.

"Here's your chance, buddy." He smacked Jack's chest. "Don't blow it. Tell her the scoop on her first husband—now's a good time if you haven't—and try and come up with other reasons as to why you want to marry her."

Jack rolled his eyes. "If she doesn't call a cab first."

Rory threw back his head, roared with laughter then left the men's room, and the event.

Jack returned to Rose's side and took a vacant seat next to her at her table.

She looked over his shoulder and asked, "Where's Rory?"

"Had to leave."

"What! But he should have taken me with him and home."

"Said no sense cutting the lovely evening short since he had to leave to pick up Angela at the hospital. Her car broke down."

"Oh, that's too bad. Well, I guess I'd better get my wrap and snatch a cab."

She started to stand up when he pressed down on her shoulder. "Sit down, sweetheart. I'll take you home when I'm ready to leave."

"But *I'm* ready now," she said.

"Let's dance a few more then we can leave."

She sighed. "All right."

Soon they were at the coat check and out of the building. They waited out front for the valet to bring Jack's car around.

He settled her into the passenger seat then got in the driver seat and started driving. And thinking. He wanted to talk to her about Timothy, and now was as good a time as any. He drove, making his way to his apartment. He'd never taken her to his place before and because he wanted to control this scene with her it would be the best place to go instead of her house.

He glimpsed the frown on her face. "Where are we going?"

"To my place," he said softly.

"No, Jack, you promised to take me home."

"We need to talk about several things, and it seems other than the few times I've been at your house we haven't had any privacy or opportunity. You trust me, right?"

"Yes, I just don't…well, I don't trust—"

"Is it because you don't trust yourself to be alone with me?"

"Of course not," she said, her eyes narrowing.

"Sure," he said dryly. "Your pride won't allow you to be honest. Tough luck, sweetheart, but we're going to my place.

When we get there call the sitter and tell her you won't be home for a few more hours."

"Do I have any choice in the matter?" she said softly.

He narrowed his eyes on her for a while and finally replied, "Not this time."

CHAPTER 16

They arrived at the apartment complex where he lived. He saw Rose take in her surroundings.

"I remember checking out these apartments before Timothy left for the war."

"But you decided to buy the house instead?"

"I don't own the house but rent it from an older couple who decided to move into a smaller place, yet they didn't want to sell their house."

"Ah," he said as he parked in his garage stall and helped her out of the car. He kept his arm around her as he guided her up the walkway to the front door.

Jack's place was on the main floor with a patio, which he appreciated, but he would be happier once he could build his own place in the development. He would need a house for Rose and Sarah.

Inside, he hung up their coats in the hallway closet.

"No Christmas tree yet?" Rose asked as she settled on his sofa while he made them a drink.

Jack shrugged. "Christmas is still two weeks away. I have time to pick one up but been too busy. I Imagine you have yours up already?"

Moving to the small liquor cabinet in one corner of the kitchen, he pulled out several bottles and made them each a drink. He already drew up plans to build his house, a Colonial style with five bedrooms and two bathrooms, and triple car garage. He also built in plans for a full-length bar in the basement family room. He'd already purchased an acre lot in the northern suburbs, close to Horizon's development so he and Rose would have a shorter drive to work. Even though Grand Horizon's development was nearly filled by home purchasers he hoped to buy more land in the general area.

Rose laughed. "Right after Thanksgiving this year. Sarah was too excited to wait."

"I understand kids and Christmas." He handed over a drink to her.

She took a sip and smiled. "What is this and in such a fancy glass. It's not a martini is it?"

"No, it's called a Sidecar, made with cognac and orange liqueur."

"I like it."

He saw her take another sip, decided to allow her to finish half the drink before bringing up Timothy. She should be more relaxed by then.

They talked about everyday things then, how her job was and if she liked it. She said she did.

He finished his sidecar, a drink too sweet for him he decided and poured himself bourbon on the rocks before settling down next to her once more.

He turned sideways and saw she'd finished her drink. "Another?" he asked.

She shook her head. "No. So what did you want to talk to me about?"

Jack took her glass and set it on the coffee table in front of them, trying to decide how to tell her. Even though he'd rehearsed it in his mind in the past he decided there'd be no stalling, no embellishing and just give her the facts.

"I hired a private investigator to see if he could find Timothy. His name is Paul Arends and he has exceptional qualifications and finds in his record."

She gasped and settled one hand on her breast. His gaze followed her hand and wished it was his hand that settled there. "First I contacted the army. They said a Timothy Dalton had lived in Minnesota, but they had no idea where he was now. There were several others in other states but they all dead-ended. The only one left was a Timothy Dalton in Alabama and that's when Arends decided to pay him a visit in person."

He took another drink, saw her eyes were wide and she sounded impatient when she said, "And?"

"He met up outside your husband's apartment and confronted him. They went to a local saloon and talked. It seems that your husband only knew his own name because upon waking in a Honolulu hospital, he was given his possessions which included dog tags, a driver license and birth certificate among other papers. Problem was he couldn't remember who he was."

"Arends had a copy of your marriage license. He showed it to Timothy, and he was shocked, but verified his signature. He had suffered a head injury at Pearl Harbor. After spending a month in the hospital, upon his release, he ended up with one of the nurses who cared for him—he married her."

"Oh, my God," Rose breathed. "So he's married to both of us."

"Afraid so. He told Arends that he wants you to divorce him. He doesn't remember you, was stunned to learn he has a daughter, but he doesn't want her to know about him and he doesn't want to meet her or you in person. It would just be too difficult, not to mention his wife is pregnant with their first child."

She sniffed. "So he doesn't want to be married to me any longer?" she asked.

He shook his head, captured a lock of her hair and pushed it behind her, then stroked her head. "Sorry, sweetheart, but in a way it's for the best, don't you think? He said it would be like being married to a stranger. He has no memory of his life before entering the service, and likely may not ever remember. He did volunteer though to pay you child support."

Rose shook her head. "No sense in that. It's just money," she sighed.

"I agree. I have his number so you can call him, talk to him about what you want to do."

"I'll divorce him, of course. Truthfully, we barely knew each other, having met just a month before he enlisted, married quickly and then he was gone the day after. He's right. We really don't know each other."

"I think that's the right thing to do," Jack said. "Now, let's talk about us. You have been avoiding us, in nearly every way you can, based on the excuse you were married to Timothy. Now that you'll be divorcing him soon, I still haven't changed my mind. I want to marry you."

"For more than the inheritance? Did you ever discover why you want to marry me other than that?" She sniffed, met his gaze.

He growled, "I told you being my wife and having children are the two most important reasons, not to mention the inheritance, but there is something else, and I think this will change your mind about me and my reasons."

"What something else?" she asked.

Jack moved right next to her, leaned down and kissed her swiftly. He hugged her close and he was pleased she didn't stiffen up and pull away.

"I believe actions say more than words," he replied, "so here's what I'll do. Once we marry and I receive the inheritance, I won't use it, but will place it into a family account for our children's education. But since you will be an at-home wife, and won't be bringing in income, then I would like an agreement from you that if my business suffers, which I don't expect it to, that we be able to use some of that money to keep it going, though we are already experiencing success and don't expect that to happen."

"Yes!" she exclaimed, a grin forming on her sweet lips.

"Is that yes to the agreement and to marrying me too?" he asked hopefully.

Nodding, she wound her arms around his neck and kissed him until all he could think about was taking her right there on his sofa. But he had other ideas in mind—better ones. He released her, stood up and scooped her into his arms.

Walking down a hallway he kept kissing her and when he settled her on his bed she said, "One last thing we need to settle."

He sank down on the bed beside her. "What's that?"

"I want to keep working at Grand Horizon Homes with you, until I am ready to have our first child. I just can't imagine staying home and taking care of a house and not much else. Are you okay with that?"

"You know this isn't my first choice but I know how important this is to you so I'll say yes, but know that truly, I expect us to have a traditional marriage, with me as head of household. It's what I've always wanted and expected in a wife. I have always believed a woman's place is in the home. Let me take care of you."

"My place will be in the home once we have child number 1..." she insisted. "I truly don't want someone else raising our children."

"Agreed. And I wear the pants," he insisted.

"I suppose, but remember that cute pair I modeled for one that one time? I think I looked pretty darned good in them," she insisted.

As Jack slowly undressed his wife to be he said, "You did —you do—but I like you best this way."

She sighed as he removed all her clothes. "Of course you do."

Late March 1948

Christmas passed quickly and Rose began planning their wedding for Saturday, May 1. While she had wanted to keep it small, Jack's parents overruled her. And because they were new in her life and her own parents were deceased, she didn't have the guts to stand up to them, even though Jack said he'd support whatever decision she came to as to size and scope of the wedding. But Jack's mother was a lovely person and since she didn't have a daughter, how could Rose refuse her help in planning a wedding? Rose could use the help.

Now she sat in the Campbell household with Jeanne Campbell, Jack's mother, as they worked on the wedding guest list. She felt some accomplishment that they'd agreed on no more than 200 guests—which was big to Rose's mind, especially since she had such a small family and had very few friends. Most of the guests would be from Jack's family and friends and work staff. They had decided on the florist, caterer, and the hall, the St. Paul Hotel, in a magnificent ballroom. They would marry at St. John's Episcopal Church, Rose's parish, just a few blocks from her house.

Sarah was at Barb's house playing with Mary so it was a relaxing time for Rose with no child interruptions. Jack sat in the living room with his father, drinking beer, watching wrestling on the TV and talking about Grand Horizon Homes.

"Well, Jack, I must say I'm impressed. You got into the housing building boom at the right time. With all of the soldiers home now, marrying and having families, they're all looking for starter homes. Great idea!"

"You—you actually paid me a compliment, Dad," Jack stated, stunned.

"I admit when you got your architecture degree, I wasn't sure what in the hell you would do for a career with it. But I always knew the banking accountant job wasn't a career for you."

"Uh, become an architect, Dad," Jack said dryly.

"I meant working in the steel industry with that degree, but you have proven yourself, son. I'm proud of you."

Jack gulped, amazed and moved by his father's compliment. John Campbell, Sr. was not lush with compliments to anyone, and definitely not to him.

"You going to expand to another development once this one is full?"

"I plan on it," Jack said, "but not until almost all lots have sold and houses built. Now that I have a family, I plan on spending as much as I possibly can with them."

His father waved his hand negligently. "You have your whole life with them to be with them. Now's the time to forge forward with your business."

Jack opened his mouth to let his dad know that he didn't want to live the life his father had, not being around much for the family, when his mother spoke up.

"Dear, Jack will run his business and his life as he sees fit, and the way he wants to. He isn't you. How many times have I told you that?"

Thank you, Mom.

The next morning, Rose found herself sick, hanging over the toilet. This was the third morning in a row Rose felt this ill and now she was beginning to doubt she had the flu. She might assume that if she'd never been pregnant before, but since she had, and she was feeling the same way when pregnant with Sarah she groaned as she sat on the bathroom floor.

She knew she had only herself to blame, consenting to making love with Jack and them not using any protection, and while they were soon marrying and would have children, she was stunned it happened as quickly as it had. But then she grimaced, thinking about how with Timothy it took only her wedding night...

"Damn, damn, damn," she whispered under her breath.

Counting back the days to her last period, which she'd missed seven weeks ago, which put her at around early February that she'd gotten pregnant, she knew now she'd have to have her wedding dress altered and pray no one would guess she was pregnant. May 1 would mean she'd be three months along. With some good wedding dress alterations, since the dress was a vintage, 20's style gown with drop waistline anyway, no one would be able to tell, though she couldn't dispute people would talk come November when she delivered a baby.

She was happy now that she'd followed Jack's instructions and filed for divorce during the week after he reported to her about Timothy. That was one big thing out of her way, for certain. She felt unencumbered and her guilt fled upon receiving her freedom from Timothy and she could now marry Jack with a free conscience.

CHAPTER 17

A week before the wedding an accounting firm, Randolph Accounting, offered Rose a job as head accountant. The irony was that she hadn't applied for the job, but someone from the bank recommended the accounting firm contact Rose, raving about her talents and that she was the best at the job.

She didn't even have to go through the interview process. They simply offered her the job, hoping she'd accept it. She did, basing her decision on several factors: due to the location, being close to her home in St. Paul where she and Jack decided they'd continue to live until they built their own home. The pay scale which Jack's company couldn't match, and the hours, which were 9-4, a bit less than the typical forty hours a week but she would be around more for Sarah before and after school.

The only kink in the ointment so to speak was the fact she was pregnant and felt it only fair to let the company know. It didn't bother them at all, and they waved the rule of allowing her to work until her 4th month, which wasn't all that far away. They said she could work until end September, five weeks before her delivery date. Not only was this unusual, but unheard of for these times. The other kink was letting Jack know. She decided the best way to do that was put in her two-week notice without telling him—she'd let Greg and Rory know, of course, and then, after they married, she'd discuss it with him.

Then she started thinking how very soon she'd also need to tell him she was pregnant, too.

Also, she decided she needed a car, not for work, but for grocery shopping, doctor appointments and other errands she'd need to do. She'd never driven before, never felt the need, but she'd be working different hours than Jack and she knew she couldn't expect him to always be available for a ride. She'd still take the streetcar to work and home but for other appointments it would just be convenient for her to have a license and car. This wasn't the first time she'd thought about it. She hoped Jack would be willing to teach her to drive—if he allowed it in the first place. She sighed, wondering if she wasn't making a mistake marrying a traditional man.

Her conscience niggled at her to tell him about the job now, before the wedding, but she knew he'd tell her no. Waiting until after the wedding would be best. She was scheduled to begin the job June 1st.

Rose would soon learn her independent attitude would not be appreciated by Jack.

❄

On Friday at work, the day before Jack and Rose's wedding, Joe Crandall, one of his carpenters took him aside.

"Darn, Jack, we'll never find a good replacement for Rose, never," he said, shaking his head.

Jack grinned. "No worries, she's not leaving right away. She'll work until she's pregnant and into her fourth month or so, but that's it. So we have time, no worries."

Joe looked at him, confused. "So you mean she's not

leaving to work at Randolph's accounting firm downtown after you're married?"

"Hell, no! Where in the heck did you get that idea?"

"From Greg. He told me she's leaving here and working at Randolph's soon. Put in her notice. Damn, he did tell me not to mention it though...double damn, thought you knew." He grimaced.

Jack glanced over at Rose who was on the phone with a client. Calm, stay calm, he told himself as he tried to figure out why she'd keep this from him. But then this niggling in his head told him she purposely withheld the information because she knew he'd say no.

On the drive home he was quiet, trying to figure out how to get her to tell him.

"How was your day?" he asked finally, figuring he could draw her out.

"You saw me, one phone call after another. It'll be good to be doing other work soo—" She came to abrupt halt.

Scowling, he asked, "What other work?" He was stunned that had been easier than he'd thought, drawing the truth out of her.

"Oh, just other work," she murmured evasively.

"The job is what it is, sweetheart, and it isn't changing," he announced. "Anything else going on in that head of yours?"

She met his side gaze and bit her lip. "Well, there are a couple of things we should talk about."

"We'll talk when we get home," he said, "so you will have my full attention."

Jack knew Sarah was staying at Barb's house overnight, giving him and Rose time to get ready or the wedding the next day. Barb offered to get Sarah bathed and dressed in her flower girl dress for the wedding and would bring her home by noon as the wedding was at two.

While he spent much of his time at Rose's house he slept

at his apartment. With Sarah at home, they decided this would be best. And every other Saturday night, Rose would stay at his apartment, where they would make love, then he'd bring her home though to sleep in her own bed. He had hoped, since they hadn't been careful, that Rose would get pregnant by their wedding day but thus far Rose hadn't said anything so he could only assume she wasn't. Yet.

They arrived at Rose's house and she appeared nervous when he opened her back door and guided her inside.

"Why don't I start dinner?" she said, walking smoothly toward the kitchen.

He grabbed her hand, stopping her. "Talk first, sweetheart," he insisted.

She nodded, biting her lower lip again which drove him insane since *he* wanted to bite it. At this moment, knowing she'd kept something so important from him, he wanted to punish her—take her over his knee. They were basing this marriage on love, respect and honesty. And not just on his part. Call him old-fashioned but he expected her to obey him.

He took her hand and admired the white blouse with bow-tied neckline she wore with a slim black skirt. Her stockings were seamed up the back and her legs appeared slim and smooth in them, along with her black high heels.

"So you were saying?" he asked, lifting his brow.

She clutched her hands in front of her and continued biting her lip but said not a word. He turned sideways, pulled her against him and kissed her until she pulled back from him with tears in her eyes. She at least had stopped biting her lip.

"Why the tears?" he asked softly.

"I—I haven't told you what's been happening in my life lately."

He smiled. "We're getting married tomorrow. What else is there to tell?"

"Maybe not," she murmured.

He frowned and moved back from her a bit, still facing

her. Jack then toed off his two-tone wingtips and crossed one leg over the other knee before he sank down on the sofa and pulled her down beside him.

"What do you mean?" he asked coolly.

"I quit Horizon," she said quickly,

Scowling, he said, "You quit? When? How? And why haven't I heard about this until now?"

"A few weeks ago someone from Randolph Accounting called me and offered me a job as head accountant."

"And?"

"I took the job."

"Did you even interview?" At her nod, he asked, "When?"

"Over the phone last week."

He sighed. "And you didn't tell me because you believed I'd say you couldn't work there. That I wanted you to stay with me at Horizon."

"Yes," she whispered. Tears filled her eyes. "I really want that job," she said. "It's my line of work."

"And being my secretary isn't," he said flatly.

She shook her head and took his hand. "Please, don't be mad at me."

"So it would be back to taking the streetcar to work and home then," he said, "as I wouldn't be able to drive you since the place is in the opposite direction."

"Well, that's my plan but also, I want to buy a car."

His eyes nearly popped out of his head. "For what? You don't drive."

"No, but I could learn. I'm simply thinking ahead."

"It's not safe."

"It's not safe for you, either," she snapped. "Besides, I can't always depend on you to be available to take me to appointments and such, you know."

"Yes, you can. I own Horizon so I can take time anytime I need to. No problem. Besides, my mother doesn't drive, nor do any of my women relatives now that I think about it. It's not something women in my family do, Rose."

"I know plenty of women drive. I worked with some at the bank. Please, you can teach me."

He sighed and raked his hand through his hair.

"What is it you don't like about me taking another job and driving?"

"It has nothing to do with me, except for the fact you lied to me, and on the day before our wedding."

"I didn't lie, I just didn't tell you."

"Same thing," he snapped.

"You don't like the idea of me having any independence."

"You are one of the most independent women I know, but you're right. I'd rather you depended upon me more."

Raising her chin she said, "I've raised my daughter just fine on my own. I've held my job just fine without a man in my life too. I've done it all on my own."

"You have," he said softly, "and I'm proud of you, but the time has come for things to change, as of tomorrow. You knew before you accepted my proposal that I'm a traditional man who expects a traditional wife."

She gave him a wide-eyed look. "So does this mean you don't want to get married? Our families will be devastated."

"Oh, believe me, we're getting married, but you," he pointed his finger at her, "will never lie by omission to me. You will never lie to me, again, and I promise I will never lie to you."

"But you lied by omission, too," she snapped, "by not telling me you owned Grand Horizon Homes."

He sighed. "I did do that, and while it was wrong I needed a good secretary. Besides, as head of our household you have to trust me that when I make a decision it's the right one for us."

"So we're talking about head of household again," she sighed.

"Now then, from now on you and I will discuss things beforehand and not afterwards as we're doing now, or you will suffer the consequences." He removed his suit jacket and proceeded to roll up his sleeves as she watched him carefully.

"Consequences?" she asked, confused.

"As a consequence of what you did this time you'll suffer some good old-fashioned punishment. And I am hopeful, in future, you won't do this again."

"What?" she gasped.

Before she could protest—before she could move—he settled his hands around her waist and pulled her down over his knees. He left her skirt in place even though he wanted to raise it and give her a firm swat on bare skin.

"Jack? What are you doing?" she shrieked, kicking and twisting to escape but his hold was tight—she was going nowhere.

His hand smacked one bottom cheek, then the other. She squealed and he lowered his raised hand, stopped as guilt came over him. Damn, there had to be another way to show her he indeed wore the pants in the house. This idea might work for Greg but not for him.

He pulled her up and held her against his chest, staring down at her. "What am I doing?" he whispered, chastising himself.

"How…how could you?" she whispered.

He couldn't miss her broken-hearted tone.

"Cleared the air," he said, "but not quite in the way I wanted to."

"You mean it cleared your anger!" she shrieked scrambling to her feet. "Never again, Jack. Never," she warned.

He sank back on the sofa, his expression still stoic as he watched her straighten her skirt and tuck her blouse back inside the waistband.

Abruptly, he rose, grabbed his jacket and headed toward

the door. He paused there and sighed as he saw her face still showed surprise and anger. "Keep the job you want. We'll see about driving this summer. And I'll see you at the church tomorrow." He left her house, paused on the stoop when something crashed against the door and his shoulders slumped.

Damn, he could only hope she showed up.

CHAPTER 18

May 1948

Jack and Rose's wedding day arrived, sunny but cool.

Rose stood before her mirror putting the final touches on her make-up. She'd spent the morning at the hairdresser who managed to coerce her hair into a smooth, elegant style. Muriel at the shop had done a beautiful job taming it so it curled softly in a long page boy style, the sides she'd put up in victory rolls. On top of it, once she got to the church, she'd gently place her tiara veil.

Her eyes were happy and clear, amazing due to how her day ended yesterday with Jack. There was no doubt in her mind he'd been furious with her. But for some reason, his light punishment seemed to clear her mind and head and she saw his point as well. Initially she'd been furious he would treat her little better than a child but in hindsight, she knew she'd disappointed him greatly, and she deserved being punished. She had to admit she was surprised he'd ended the punishment so quickly, and it was worth it since he informed her she could keep the new job and he might teach her to drive. Those two swats were worth it, she mused, thoroughly satisfied.

Smiling to herself as she stood up from her vanity table, he likely figured she wouldn't be showing up for the wedding today, though she wouldn't put it past him to retrieve her if she didn't.

She also admitted he'd made her feel loved and protected with those few 'love taps'. But no more of that treatment would she tolerate, yet she promised she'd obey him from now on, though she knew she wouldn't stop trying to get her way, in particular, learning how to drive.

She dressed in her one pair of black pants and a lightweight floral top when she heard the doorbell ring. Glancing down at her watch she realized that had to be Barb coming by with Sarah.

She opened the door and tears filled her eyes at her pretty little girl, dressed in a hot pink frilly flower girl dress in a bouffant style, her hair with a big pink ribbon in it.

"Don't you look beautiful!" she exclaimed, grinning down at Sarah.

"Pink, Momma. Why do I have to wear pink?" her little tomboy said with a scowl.

"You look beautiful in pink and you match your aunts who will be wearing pink bridesmaid dresses."

Pink wasn't really Rose's color either, but Jack's mom begged her to choose the color for Sara and her sisters. How could she say no, especially since they also insisted on paying for the entire wedding. Which was a good thing since Rose had very little extra money.

"Thanks so much, Barb. And you look beautiful!"

Barb smiled down at her pale-yellow shift dress and matching coat. "I haven't been to a wedding in so long I am looking forward to it. And just getting Charlie into a suit these days is difficult so this was the perfect excuse. Come on, he's ready to take us to the church."

At the church they all made their way to the bride dressing room. Miriam and Elaine were there already.

"It's about time you got here," Miriam exploded.

Glancing at her watch again, Rose said, "But it's only 1:30."

"And you're getting married in half an hour," Elaine said. "Your groom has been here nearly two hours."

"I wonder why?" Rose mused aloud, grinning to herself. "I've got plenty of time," Rose added. She pointed to her hair and face. "See, I had my hair done this morning and put on my makeup."

"How did you get to the hairdressers? Don't tell me you took the streetcar early this morning."

Rose laughed and said, "No, meet Barb, my next-door neighbor—no—more than my neighbor. She's a friend and a godsend."

"Oh, pshaw," Barb said. "I'll go tell Jack you've arrived and put him out of his misery."

The women all laughed at that remark.

Within a short time, after her sisters primped her, she was dressed in her vintage style dress with a short train and long veil and tiara. Miriam handed her a bouquet of white roses with trailing vines and a pink ribbon—it was beautiful Rose thought and sighed. Her hand shook slightly as she held the bouquet and, with her sisters holding the short train, they made their way to the back of the church to walk up the aisle.

The double doors leading into the church were shut so they got in position, waiting for one of the ushers to open the doors. Then she smiled when Jack's father appeared from another room on the opposite side of the hallway from where she'd dressed.

"About time you got here, darlin'," he said, grinning widely down at her. It struck her then how much Jack did resemble his father, who'd been delighted she'd asked him to walk her down the aisle.

"Why is everyone worried about me showing up on time?" she whispered.

He wiggled his eyebrows. "From what my son tells me, he was the one worried you might not show up. Did you two have a fight?"

"A bit of one yesterday," she admitted, "but we straightened things out."

"Glad to hear it," he intoned lowly, looking at her from head to toe. Then he sighed. "You make one beautiful bride, Rosie, that's for sure. You'll knock his socks off, as they say down south."

He was the only one that got away with calling her Rosie. She'd long given up on correcting him.

Organ music could be heard as an usher opened the doors. The organist started playing *Here Comes the Bride*, and Rose's sisters walked down the aisle first, meeting up with Greg and Rory up near the altar, their husbands in the pew where they'd be sitting. Greg's wife was there in the same row but across from the other, along with Rory's girlfriend.

Rose started trembling and Jack's father must have felt it for he pulled her close and patted her hand over his arm as they slowly made their way down the aisle. Rose looked straight ahead, a small smile on her face then, meeting Jack's intent stare. He never moved his gaze from her all the way down the aisle until she reached him. Then his lips broke out in that charming smile of his and she grinned back. She saw how Jack's eyes welled with tears and she sniffed her own away.

His father kissed her cheek and handed her over to Jack, who took her hand and pulled her flush against his side as the pastor began the ceremony.

Rose couldn't help looking at him, seeing how handsome he looked in his black wedding suit, a tuxedo with satin lapels, white shirt and tie, a small pink boutonniere on one lapel.

The pastor said, "Who gives this woman to this man?"

Sarah jumped up from her seat in the first pew and said, "Me, her daughter Sarah."

The entire congregation of guests laughed and applauded.

Soon Jack and Rose recited their wedding vows. Upon much discussion beforehand, Jack had agreed that 'obey' in the vows wasn't important for Rose to say, so he was surprised when she said hers, after he gave his vow, and tears filled his eyes again.

"I, Rose Marie, take you, Jack Robert , to be my husband, to have and to hold from this day forward; for better, for worse, for richer, for poorer, in sickness and in health, to love, cherish, and obey, till death us do part, according to God's holy law."

They presented rings, matching gold bands to each other and as Jack slid hers on, followed by her engagement ring, he couldn't help but lean down and kiss her lips gently, much to everyone's surprise since this wasn't the place where the groom should kiss his bride. But that was Jack, uncaring of convention, and Rose loved him more for it.

Soon the service ended, and they walked arm in arm down the aisle and out the door, standing outside in the receiving line to meet their guests. Since they were the first ones out of the church, they talked quietly to each other before anyone else appeared.

"Thank you," Jack said softly, kissing her cheek.

"For what?" Rose looked at him quizzically.

"For showing up. For marrying me. For making me the happiest man in the world."

She grinned. "Don't think I hadn't thought about not showing, believe me."

He gulped and she saw the tears in his eyes. "I should not have—done what I did. Never again," he promised.

Just then the wedding party appeared, and she whispered, "Talk later."

He nodded and they shook hands and exchanged hugs with their wedding attendants and guests. Sarah grabbed onto Jack's hand and he whisked her up into his arms. She whispered to him, "Can I call you Daddy?"

He nodded. "I would be proud if you would."

Rose heard his choked tone and smiled, knowing she'd made the right decision, for Jack, for her and for Sarah.

It was a long, emotional, fun-filled day for Rose and Jack and finally, when the wedding ended at one o'clock in the morning, they made their way in the elevator up to their suite in the hotel.

Jack unlocked the door. Rose made to cross the threshold when Jack hauled her up into his arms. "You know the tradition, sweetheart," he purred, and she laughed as he carried her into their suite.

Within moments of entering, Jack had Rose get out of her beautiful gown and veil and into a negligee that was white and see-through. He sat on the sofa in the living area. He'd held a glass of champagne in one hand and twirled his pointer finger with the other when she left their bedroom and came toward him.

Rose gave him a dimpled smile she knew he loved and turned when Jack ordered, "Stop."

He could see through her gown and she guessed what he was looking at and she blushed to the roots of her hair for she felt the heat sear her body.

"So glad I didn't leave any marks. I owe you an apology, darling," he said lowly, his voice gruff.

"Apology accepted," she said softly.

He gulped and leaned forward, took her hand and sat her on his lap. "Why did you put obey back in our vows when we decided we wouldn't have it?"

"Because I wanted to prove to you I'd never lie again or by omission do so, either, so it had to be a vow from me, given freely from my heart. Now, then, I have just one more teensy thing to confess now."

He sighed, slumped low on the sofa and closed his eyes. "Now what? I already told you to keep the accounting job and soon I'll begin giving you driving lessons, heaven help me."

She squealed in excitement. "Oh, my gosh, I am so exited!"

"So," he said, narrowing his eyes, "what's the other teensy thing?"

"I'm…I'm expecting."

He shot up so quickly he almost knocked her off his lap. He looked her up and down with wide eyes and he had her two hands and held her in front of him, then slid one hand carefully over her stomach.

"You're truly pregnant?" he asked, his voice filled with worry and a dash of excitement.

"Yes," she whispered, leaned forward and kissed him.

Jack wound his hand through her hair and fisted it, pulling her lush frame against his chest. "How far?"

"About three months."

"Have you been to a doctor yet?"

"No, because I just finally realized I was pregnant last week. When we return from Niagara Falls, I'll make an appointment."

He cleared his throat and looked away from her.

She frowned. "What's wrong?"

"You might not realize it, but I was hoping you'd get pregnant sooner than later."

She laughed. "Of course I knew that, and it's what I wanted also. You have made me a happy woman, Jack."

"And I am an ecstatic husband," he growled as he took her in his arms.

CHAPTER 19

Two months later

Jack waited anxiously, looking out the window of the home he'd purchased for his new family.

The home was located a short distance from the Horizon development. It wasn't brand new but ten years old —an interim home for them since he'd be building them a brand-new home in his next development which they'd begin in a year.

Rose wasn't home from work yet and he was worried, praying she hadn't been in an accident.

Not only had he taught her to drive but he'd purchased her a1946 Ford Super DeLuxe Tudor sedan in white. Since the week following their wedding, she'd been working as an accountant at Randolph's and she loved the job, which didn't make him happy. But he also knew within a few months she would be leaving that position, per the company's rules regarding pregnant women; at seven months pregnancy she would have to leave. By late September she'd be done working and would be at home where he wanted his wife to be. Or, if she truly wanted to continue working longer she could work for his company again.

He breathed a relieved sigh when he saw her coming down the street and carefully pulled into the driveway. Truth be told he thought she drove better than he did—well, she was cautious and drove the speed limit, unlike him, though he was trying to be more conscientious about it.

He walked out the door to greet her. He'd left work early today as this was their two-month wedding anniversary and they had dinner plans at a new steak house in downtown. He was dressed and ready to go. All Rose needed to do was change her clothes. Sarah was staying with her new friend next door.

Jack stood on the stoop and frowned when he noticed Rose's stooped shoulders. She looked beat—really beat. He started down the stairs.

"Everything okay, darling?" he asked.

She stopped in front of him, her purse clutched over her arm as she looked up at him and tears filled her eyes.

"What's wrong?"

She simply stood there, shaking her head and he gathered her into his arms when she started bawling. He let her cry without speaking, holding her tight against him. If her boss had been a jerk to her he'd hear from him—more than hear. He'd punch the guy if he did something to hurt Rose.

Finally, she stepped back, and he guided her up the stairs and inside. She still hadn't said a word but sniffed as she tried to control her sobbing.

Jack guided her to the sofa and settled her down beside him.

"Tell me what happened?"

She smoothed down the skirt of her floral summer dress with full skirt, no seamed waistline since she was pregnant. It had short sleeves and a scooped neck—he loved this dress on her because she looked pretty, small, except for her well-rounded stomach, and utterly feminine in it.

"I—I—got fired," she cried, then sank her head against his chest as she started crying again in earnest.

"What the hell?" he growled. "Why?"

"Because I'm, I'm pregnant!"

"Well, of course you are, and Randolph knew it. He said you could work until September."

She shook her head against his chest. "Oh, he had every right to let me go, I guess."

"Why is that when he promised you September?"

"Because this baby has grown so big already and it's pressing on my bladder so I spent a lot of time in the ladies," she murmured.

Grinning, he kept his head high, not wanting her to see his expression. "But he knew this would happen, didn't he?"

She sniffed, raised her head, her eyes still filled with tears. "Yes, but he said other pregnant employees never spent as much time in the ladies and that I'd have to leave." Scowling, she added, "And I know I'm much bigger earlier with this baby than I'd been with Sarah."

Since he went to every doctor appointment each month he knew this was true as her doctor mentioned it. There was no telling what the baby's sex was, but he hoped it was a boy, yet another daughter would please him also.

"You know, you don't need to work," he said and smiled down at her. "And maybe Sarah would like you to be home with her more now anyway."

"You think so? I know Barb has been great taking care of her while we're at work so maybe she could use a break."

"I'm sure she could. And you and Sarah could spend the next months before the baby's born just having some fun together, until school begins in September."

Rose sniffed and smoothed her skirts down, pausing with her hands over her growing stomach. "You're right. It would give us some time together, and we could do some fun things, too."

"Absolutely, enjoy the rest of summer. You could also get some rest in as well." Leaning forward he looked down at her feet. "I noticed lately your ankles are swelling more. You need rest, darling."

"I think so, too," she whispered, her head on his shoulder. "Please don't be mad at me but it'll take me some time getting used to being a regular housewife at home."

"Of course it will."

She lifted her head and she pressed her lips against his.

His heart raced as she kissed him, enchanted with his new wife all over again. From the day he saw her on that street corner he'd felt overwhelming attraction for her, and that certainly hadn't changed. He rubbed her swelling stomach and his heart ached with love for her.

She ended the kiss and she whispered, "Do you mind if we stay home tonight? I just don't feel up to going out."

"No problem. Why don't I go down the street and pick up some burgers for us from Sunny's?"

"Oh, that sounds marvelous."

Mid-October 1948

The October sun shone down on Rose where she relaxed in her back yard on a lounge chair. The weather was unseasonably warm, and Rose loved it. Every day of warmth meant a shorter winter to her mind. After losing her job at Randolph's she admitted she was glad now; her body and mind needed a rest.

Her swollen ankles had gone down even as her belly kept growing. She was being careful about what she ate, staying away from too much salt, and at twenty-nine, as her doctor mentioned, she was no spring chicken having this baby. Still, she felt so much better being home, taking care of herself and unborn child. Never had she believed she'd be able to lead such a life of luxury and relaxation.

Jack was a wonderful, caring husband who insisted she rest. She could always come back to work part time after the baby was born for Grand Horizon Homes he'd said, if she wished.

Sarah skipped out of the house and headed toward her with a glass of lemonade sloshing in her hand.

"Careful, Sarah," Rose called out.

"Sorry, Mommy," Sarah said as she handed over the tall glass. "I need to get over to Mimi's house." Excitement filled her voice. "We'll be putting on a play for you and her mom later today!"

"Oh, of course you will," Rose said with a smile. "Just let me know what time to come over to watch and thank you for the lemonade."

Smiling, she watched her daughter skip away next door, thinking how Sarah was growing up and since moving into this house she'd made a few good little friends. Sarah had been so sad to leave their first house since Mary, her best friend, lived there but Rose made sure she saw her often. Seven years old already and she'd started second grade last month. Rose sighed, thinking how time passed quickly.

She tipped her floppy brimmed hat over her face and dozed in the sun peacefully until a cramp started in her stomach. Frowning, she sat up and shoved the hat off her head and smoothed a hand over her stomach.

Darn bowels, she mused, thinking about what she'd eaten today that might have caused this dull ache. Cereal this morning and a ham sandwich at lunch—nothing else so it couldn't be food.

She jiggled her position in the lounge chair a bit, donned her hat again and closed her eyes. Soon she sat upright once more when a harder pain struck her. As she struggled to get out of the chair she thought a trip to the bathroom was a good idea.

Rose slowly made her way inside, tossed her hat on the kitchen table and rubbed her stomach as she made her way to the bathroom. She glanced down at her watch, glad to see it was nearly three and Jack said he'd be home early today. A good thing since she was a bit worried.

As she entered the bathroom she gasped at the pain and bent over, holding onto the sink. Breathing in and out, trying to regulate her breathing as she handled the growing ache in her stomach she knew something wasn't right, guessing this baby was coming two months early!

She closed the bathroom door, raised her maternity dress, tugged down her briefs and sank down on the toilet. She felt the baby move and breathed a sigh of relief that all was well, and she likely had a strong case of gas. After relieving herself she rose from the toilet, wiped herself and saw blood and her heart raced. Oh, God, this baby *was* coming early. Her hands shook as she reached inside the cabinet and found a sanitary pad and belt just as she heard the front door open.

"I'm home, Rose! Where are you?"

The boisterous sound of Jack's voice calmed her, and she called back, "Um, honey, can you come here?"

She stood in the hallway outside the bathroom as he came around the corner and headed toward her, frowning as he looked down at her hands clutching her stomach.

He took her shoulders and saw tears in her eyes.

"I think the baby's coming," she whispered.

"Too early," he said.

"I'm bleeding."

"We're going to the hospital."

She heard his calm reply and sighed, knowing she could depend on him to be strong and sensible.

After Jack consulted with Mimi's mother who said she'd

keep Sarah with her until she heard back from him, he whisked Rose into the car and to the hospital.

Forty minutes later, after the hospital staff had gotten Rose settled into a bed in the maternity-delivery section, her doctor arrived.

Rose was having contractions now and her brow was slick with moisture from her laboring. She held onto Jack's hand tightly until a contraction eased away, then her doctor spoke.

Dr. Winstead stood beside the bed on one side, Jack on the other.

"It appears this baby wants to come early, Rose and Jack. But he or she seems to be of a viable weight, so there shouldn't be distress for the baby. But I will say that for you, Rose, I don't think you'll be able to deliver normally due to the size of the baby."

"I know you mentioned that at Rose's last visit," Jack said. "But since she'd be delivering early do you think that opinion still stands?"

"Yes, I do. All along this baby has been larger than the average. I'm afraid a cesarian section will need to be done."

"Oh," Rose whispered, clutching her stomach.

"No worries," Dr. Winstead said. "We do this type of operation often enough I don't anticipate any problems."

Rose gulped. "Alright, when will you do it?"

The doctor glanced down at his watch. "As soon as I get scrubbed up and a team gathered we'll operate." He patted her hand and added, "Everything will be fine."

"Stay with me, Jack," she begged as he walked alongside the gurney to the operating room.

"Sorry, an orderly said, but dads need to stay in the waiting room."

"No," Rose said. "He's coming in with me!"

At the operating room doors, the orderlies opened them and blocked Jack from entering.

"I want my husband with me!" Rose exclaimed, turning to find her doctor already in the room.

"Rose, this is irregular, especially for an operation. If he were a doctor it might be different but he's not," her doctor warned.

"I know my wife," Jack said staunchly, "and I know I can handle this."

Dr. Winstead looked Jack over carefully and finally nodded. "Have you ever seen blood?"

Jack nodded. "Yes. I was a medic in the war."

"Oh! You never told me that!" Rose exclaimed.

Grinning down at her, he said, "I will if you want to hear about it."

She nodded. "I do."

"But Dr. Winstead," a nurse said, "this is highly irregular."

"It might be, but Mr. Campbell can handle it. I'm sure he saw his fair share of injuries during the war as a medic." He eyed Jack once more, head to toe. "Put on a gown and cap, then move up around to your wife's head, Jack, and hold her hand until we put her under."

"I love you," Rose whispered as the anesthetist placed a mask over her nose and told her to count back from one-hundred.

Jack sat in a corner in Rose's hospital room, in a large cushioned chair, one leg crossed over his knee, a baby settled in the space—a good sized baby, for his son had weighed in at seven pounds, eight ounces and was twenty-two inches long. He grinned as he looked down at him. He sighed, knowing Dr. Winstead made the correct decision in taking the baby for Jack doubted if his small wife could have delivered normally, and for sure she wouldn't have if she'd gone full-term.

He and Rose had discussed names, but they hadn't definitively decided. He was partial to Liam while Rose liked Conor, and now he decided, since Rose had done the hard work, Conor Liam Campbell he'd be called.

The baby had been sleeping mostly since birth and Jack now waited in Rose's room for her to wake from the anesthesia in a recovery room. It was taking longer than usual but nothing to worry about Dr. Winstead explained.

He looked up when the door opened and the gurney with Rose on it was pushed into the room.

Jack rose quickly and set the baby down in the small, ambulatory bed for him then moved to Rose's side. She appeared to be asleep yet. "Has she awakened yet?"

The nurse who accompanied the orderlies replied, "Yes, slowly coming out of it. She's a bit groggy yet but she knows her name and where she's at." The nurse grinned at Jack and added softly, "You can tell her the good news."

Jack nodded. "Thanks for saving that for me. I appreciate it."

"No problem," she said, then they all left.

Jack moved to the bed, dropped the side down and sat next to Rose. Her eyes were still closed so he picked up her hand and kissed it, looking down on the most beautiful woman he'd ever seen, proud to claim her as his wife.

Slowly she opened her eyes, looked into his and smiled. She started to sit up and she gasped, her eyes widening, but he held her down. "Lay there and I'll bring the head of the bed up," he said. At her nod he did exactly that then sat down beside her again.

"It'll take time," he said softly, "but your tummy will be sore for a while."

She frowned as she looked around the room and her eyes

focused on the small bed on a tall frame. Then she gasped, "Oh! I had the baby!"

"You sure did, sweetheart," he said, then chuckled.

"Boy or girl?" she asked.

"Yes. I spoke with the nurse while you were still under and she said we need to place a pillow on your tummy first. Let me fetch one."

He moved to the closet in a corner and pulled out another pillow and settled it on her stomach. Then he turned and rolled the small bed to her side. She started to reach for him when Jack stopped her with a hand on her shoulder.

Scowling, he said, "I know this is going to be hard for you to stay a bit quieter than you're used to, but you must. You don't want to tear open any stitches, okay?" At her nod he added, "I'll pass him to you."

"We have…we had a boy?" she said softly.

"I'll say, seven pounds eight ounces."

"Oh, my gosh." Her eyes widened on their son as Jack settled him onto the pillow and her arms came around him. "Sarah only weighed five pounds."

They sat together, admiring their baby. Jack helped her hold the baby as they talked over names once more. He'd made Rose happy at the decision to go with Conor Liam.

"Sarah wanted to come down to see him," Jack said, "but hospital rules say only adults."

Tears filled Rose's eyes. "I miss her. How long will I be here?"

Jack hated hearing the tremble in her voice but smiled and reassured her. "Too long but necessary. You'll be here another five days, possibly seven depending upon your recovery."

"Oh! That's a long time. I've never been away from Sarah for any length of time."

"I already spoke with her and while she's sad she understands you need to heal. Your sister, Miriam, arrived today and she's taking care of Sarah until you come home. We have a wonderful daughter, and now a son."

Rose nodded and started crying in earnest.

Jack gasped, "What's wrong, honey? You'll see Sarah soon, and—"

"Oh, I cried off and on the first month after I had Sarah. My doctor said it was hormone imbalance."

"Over nothing you cried?" he asked incredulously.

"Over everything!" she announced and laughed then, even as tears filled her eyes and Jack laughed along.

Jack leaned forward and kissed her hard, one arm around her and one around the baby. When he lifted his head she gave him a quizzical look.

"What was that for?"

"To make you stop crying, of course."

EPILOGUE

Christmas eve 1948

Jack and Rose sat on the sofa, staring at the twinkling lights on their Christmas tree, deep in thought as they drank wine.

"You do know today was my official due date to have Conor, don't you?" Rose asked.

Jack nodded. "Sure do. Conor decided otherwise, though, didn't he?"

Rose grinned. "I'll say. Hard to believe he's two months old already. And finally I'm starting to lose weight."

"Not too much weight, though, sweetheart. You were too thin to begin with. Besides, as long as you're breast-feeding Conor you need to keep weight on."

She slapped his shoulder. "Don't tell me you've been reading up on it?" At his nod and grin she sighed. "So you want to keep me fat and and pregnant, do you?"

He pulled her against him and slapped her bottom once firmly. "You are far from fat," he growled. "As for being pregnant, no. I am perfectly happy with our two kids."

"I wouldn't mind having one or two more, but we'd have

to get started immediately since I'm not getting any younger." She sighed.

Jack's eyes filled with tears. "I always wanted a big family since I'd been an only, and believe me, my parents would be so happy if we did have more, but ultimately, it's your decision if you believe you want to go through that again."

"I do," she replied.

He squeezed her tight against him. "Then we should get started soon." He cleared his throat and asked, "Has Dr. Winstead cleared you to, well, you know?"

"Yes, as of today, we are fine to make love." Pouting, she rubbed her bottom and added, "But no more of that. You promised."

"Sorry," he murmured. "Forgot."

She sniffed, "Well, a reminder swat now and then might be warranted."

He leaned back and looked down at her, his eyebrows raised. "Are you giving me permission to punish you when you need it?"

"No, not exactly, but when I'm feeling in the 'mood' I wouldn't mind a smack or two," she said softly.

He laughed loudly.

"Sh, sh, the kids are sleeping," she warned, her fingers to his mouth.

He bit her finger and she gasped.

"Are you telling me I do, after all, wear the pants in the house?"

"You always have, and you always will."

"Precisely the words I want to hear," he stated.

"Oh, but we have one more thing to discuss, darling," she murmured as she reached up and kissed his lips sweetly.

"And what's that?" He kissed her back, hard and long.

"About me returning to work for you."

Jack groaned. "Let's talk about it tomorrow, okay?"

"Sure," she said, a twinkle in her eye which he saw.

"You're not serious," he said, narrowing his eyes on her.

She laughed, jumped off the couch and ran down the hallway. He was on her heels, joining her in their bedroom where he quietly shut the door, turned the lock and took her in his arms.

"You're joking, right?" he persisted.

"What do you think?" she asked coyly.

"I say I better get you pregnant tonight."

She shrugged. "If you're up for the job."

He dragged her to the bed and started undressing her. "Let me show you…"

THE END

Don't miss out on your next favorite book!
Join the Satin Romance mailing list
www.satinromance.com/mail.html

THANK YOU FOR READING

❄

Did you enjoy this book?

We invite you to leave a review at your favorite book site, such as Goodreads, Amazon, Barnes & Noble, etc.

DID YOU KNOW THAT LEAVING A REVIEW...

- Helps other readers find books they may enjoy.
- Gives you a chance to let your voice be heard.
- Gives authors recognition for their hard work.
- Doesn't have to be long. A sentence or two about why you liked the book will do.

ABOUT THE AUTHOR

Nancy Schumacher is the owner-publisher of Melange Books, LLC, writing under the pseudonyms, Nancy Pirri and Natasha Perry.

She is a member of Romance Writers of America. She is also one of the founders of the RWA chapter, Northern Lights Writers (NLW), in Minnesota.

www.nancypirri.com

facebook.com/NancyPirriAuthor